Saint Gredible and Her Fat Dad's Mass

Saint Gredible and Her Fat Dad's Mass

Joe Panzica

Kalabram Select

Them

That burly truck driver with the nervous tic? He led armed men in partisan forests hiding children and elders safe deep under crunchy snows.

That cigar-coughing seller of death insurance? He dragged informants from their grease-smoked kitchens and punched bullets between their anguished eyes under ice-clad pines. That raccoon-eyed librarian? Following the loud sounding roundup of siblings, parents, cousins, and urine-scented grandparents, she huddled her taut frame too tightly round a smothered baby niece in an empty cistern behind a frozen coal bin until the last loose heirloom was looted by friendly neighbors from her noosed family's ransacked farm.

That saturnine shuffler? He never hurt a fly. He just survived. That laughing harridan? They murdered her first husband and brood, but is now with new issue who've spawned crawling rugrats of their own. That lanky bookseller? That anxious landlord? That chain-smoking stenographer? That vodkamouthed claims investigator? That fleshy, pigeyed greengrocer? That lipsticked Tupperware Empress? That soulful schlubby housewife?

That bespectacled nebbish who sells you magazines and

breath mints? That brash know-it-all pisk with the racing forms? That flirty matron with the papery skin? That green mascaraed Mrs. Robinson? That eye-shifting, droopy little barfly? That unshaven platform stander at the station on all the coldest dark mornings?

That sunburnt jolly beach ball thrower with sand spackled over the backside of his well-soaked Bermudas? That horse-voiced abuser of umpires two seats away in Spray Stadium? That overly distinguished gentleman who carefully offers you sports pages as he dips away from the donut counter? That flesh puffy arm with the nicotine-stained fingers below the rolled-up sleeve of the sloppy floppy green chenille sweater pushing, to untiring howls of abandoned laughter, a boisterous baby on the small children's swing-set in Roslyn Park one cloudsoft 1973 April afternoon?

And what if THEY, with undoubted secret superpowers, could, under the worse of circumstances… He never hurt a fly. He just survived. He just survived. Just survived.

Dedication

Most of all to *Sharon*.

but also to Arnie and Renata and their entire family extending back, forth, and dogward.

And to my family, especially Penay with his Kootsy, Booby, Squirrels, Rabbits, Kangaroos, Walls, and Arabian Nights.

Be it known that the stories mentioned above are all illustrated by Joseph A. Panzica Jr. (Penay) and are inspired (with the exception of Al Bak Buk) by his stories and books.

(a guide for the perplexed)

The Song of Abraham

Or The Sad Ballad of Avram the Idler

Well, they call my Kitty, BABY,
But their real name
    Their real name
        Their real name
            Their real name
is Cindy Lou!
    (And mine was too)

They're trying to creepycrawl to Whoville
But Dr. Spock
    and Mr. Seucey
        are running their wicked rackets
          deep beneath
the city zoo.
    (As droogs will do)

Well, I call my Greddy, WICKED
Cause she's
    twitching
        and itching
          and swishing
her icy brew.
    (That's coke a lawny punch to you.)

Still, you can call my Sally, silly
But he's running
            an aching migraine
                        since he wolfed down
all the yellow stew.
            (Who knew?)

                                        * * *

And You can call me Abe.
And YOU can call me Abey!
And *they* can call me Ibrahim
(cause I'm Papoosie to my baby).

You can call me Abram, Avram,
—or call me plain old Avi.
(You can call me in the desert
if you get bars in the Mojave.)

You can call me Bram though
I'm a joker, not a Stoker
(When my daughter calls me Poopie
sometimes I wanna choke her.)

I say *Avrasha*. She says Avraamy
(It's not kosher so I chew salami.)

Abrom, Avrom, Abrami
Abbaran, Ob, or Brommie
Hammy Brammy Hammy Brammy
How I love you
            How I Love you... *my drear old...*

Only Forward

The forms and structures of language (including so called "literature") are a vast legacy of riches encrusted with inspirations and temptations. They are also immense burdens that constrict and pervert our perceptions and expressions — even as they help orient us toward pinpricks of illumination into what seems (to us) to be.

As our latest "age" now crumbles and tears itself apart, we (with no secure prospect of any renaissance even in the farthest future) grapple with misleadingly vague ideas of "objective reality", "gender", "consciousness" and "personhood." None of those concerns are truly "new," because for us they have always been and will ever remain both essential and urgent while also perpetually relegated to the peripheral, the absurd, the danger-ous, and the effete.

Our legacies with their trauma, boosts, shames, and burdens do not define us any more than do our stories, but that does not mean we could live (as humans) without them. We (all) use stories as ways of forming, encasing, and protecting our fragile and incomplete "selves" even as they may also serve as tendrils guiding us toward possibly worthy potentialities. And Fab QuarterDead Dwarf Dakota MacDougle still beckons us to "IMAG-INE" our best possibilities.

If we dare... If we can...

Contents

I

Vernal Pools of New England

Simmering Summer Kills

V

Home for the Jolly Days

Vernal Pools of New England

One

The Teardrop Collider

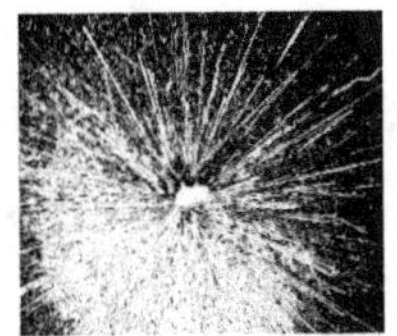

S TREAMLY Gredible careened, nearly graceful, the corner formed by the white sidewalk sloping down and the black driveway mounting up.

Striving anxiously against gravity, she pedalpushed frantically enough to gain the desired velocity for colliding energetically into the massive left shin of her gargantuan father.

Then without regret, she grinned insolently up into the wide and watery eyes of her stunned progenitor who lifted her fierceness off her board and then high above his head where he shook her quite vigorously.

She shrieked with laughter, and the arms of enormous Avram Ider tired before his shin's throbbing could begin to subside. Briskly kicking the offending skateboard into a nearby hedge, he set her gently down and groped carefully the back of her head.

Mournfully, he watched the knapsack waggle on her back as she scrambled to the house and bounced through the springing slamming door. And groaning, somewhat histrionically, he followed, shambling up the stoop.

*

Two

Skates of Matter

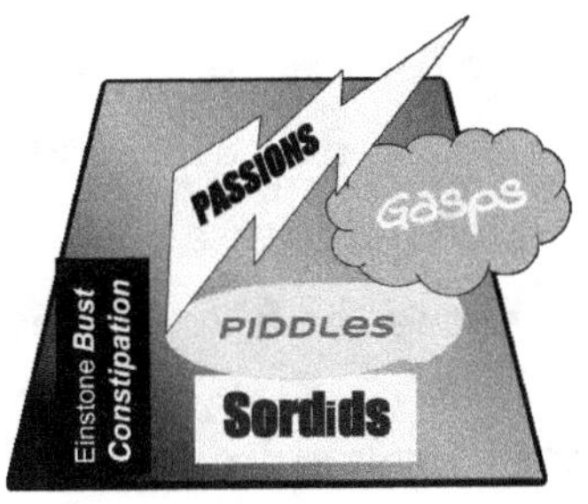

*O*BESE Abe Idler trundled wounded up the stoop and into the homely cabin of Stan and Carol Ann. He shut closed his eyes and, staggering like a blinded man, cried out thrice, "Will no one help a frightful old bookjew?" to the assseated company who all except Stan, his attenuated friend, stared back coldly.

Absorbing the silence, Abey slumped and shuffled toward the untidy table slurring, "Sumptymize it's improstate to schtup meself. Pity me. Pity me. Pity me."

High-placed Carol Ann Olgivy glared down at unlaced Stanislaw Imerese who shrugged and slabbed more butter on the remaining crumb of what was once a generous slice of fresh-baked Irish Soda Bread. "Anyway," she proclaimed, "Zlottie has this wonderful idea!"

Each female detected Abe's failure to conceal a jolt of alarm, but Ms. Olgivy, Stanley's marital mistress, primly continued. "Gretty's friend Jesse's parents backed out of a promise to take her to the Black Lives Matter March."

"Bleak lives splatter," was glum Avram's wary response.

Carol Ann sucked in her breath and held her tongue. Eyeing her, the girl, now minus the knapsack, pursed her lips to conceal a grin and then found herself examining closely her taut forearms.

Were blue-black glyphs gradually emerging from the skin there? Neither her live dud of a dad nor her dead Mudd of a mom had them yet either. Maybe you had to grow streamly old first?

Her grandfathers were sweet, sad Obbie and bad old Zeyde Zee. Both had them: numbers, dashes, and letters, smudged over by so many long dry years. Glowing through her olive blonde skin were only veins, pale blue for lack of oxygen. Reassured, she readdressed her attention to the adult company.

Grinchily she assessed each one in turn before dropping her jaw and scrunching her eyes at her offending fat dad who never got rattled like other grown-ups might. But, then again, he had taught it to her. A quick pucker crushed back his own colluding grin.

Zlottie Vimshireik prodded his fleshy forearm. "It would be good! Her. Her friend. Your friends. Us?"

Foolish Abe squirmed and whined. "When? It's gotta be a WALK? Can't we watch it on the 'lectric nintertoob like syblized people? I'll keep my fat thumb on the 'Like' button. I'll contribute to the Kool-Aid fund!"

Zlottie's eyes narrowed and then widened with old-world expressivity. "Children need experience. Genuine experience. They need friends. Both of them. They need friends and family. All children. They need community. They need fresh air and exercise."

"Exercise? I bought her the DUCKING skateboard! What if we just *rode* the march on one of dem *quack quack* semi-aquatic Fuck Tours?"

Carol Ann cocked her head. "Can't we please avoid the vocal explosions? PLEASE?"

"This is immersive education!" declared Zlottie as if that settled the matter.

"Or subversive asphyxiation..."

Carol Ann started, then stopped picking up plates. "Anyway, all grumbling aside, it's settled. Stan and I will drive to your Cambridge place. Jessie's dad will drop her off there, and we'll all make a day in the town of it."

Abe Ider pouted and gnawed a bialy.

Stanley the blessed peacemaker ventured, "So Abe, what do you think of the Hamiltonian interpretation of the 25th Amendment?"

"I think we're *enough* set with enough politics for an entire trimester or three." Abe for some time had been heavily invested in exploring additionally odd ways to modulate between the dark trembling timbre of a groan and the high lonesome plaintive of the whine.

Stanistooge graciously explained to the unfazed ladies, "Abe believes neither in individual agency nor collective determinism."

"You said we could go to the skate park by now."

Abe Ider, fully cognizant of the exasperated indifference of the bulk of his audience, eagerly assumed the ostentatious grandeur of a ponderous lecturer. "On the minnow scales of uncertain corpuscles, there are no definite skates or even sports in thyme or spice until you peer in close and spook."

"If you need to peer in this house, Care prefers you use the pisser over in there."

From its corner, the girl grabbed her skateboard. *"I wanna go again before it might rain or something."*

"Contrariwise, on the mackerel's scales, it's just the perverse."

"Carol Ann, will you take me and Zlottie?"

"There, apparently weighty concepts appear to have great estate and solidity only until you poke up close."

"It would be fun. I'm teaching me new moves." Springs in her knees bounced the girl anxiously down and up.

"And then they dissipate into vacant immateriality.

"So we're going now, right?"

"To unamerican foreigners, for example, we're all of us Yankees, however transplanted. But to any blood and soil New Englander, a Yankee is some old bachelor farmer on a mountaintop."

"It's not fair if we don't go now."

"But FIND an old yeoman in the Vermontaeon highlands! You'll probably greet a transplanted pawnbroker from Crown Heights who calls hisself Izzy Yidursky."

"And what if he's actually a NAZI?" piped in half his exasperated daughter, half sneering, half trying to please, half wishing she were somewhere else.

And then there are NAZIs," continued Abey unfazed.

"I'll just go again on my own."

"If you found one, would it be some thin-lipped, heel-clicking nihilist into S&M? Would it be some spite-dripping minion with an arsenal of AR-15s and a closet full of dancing boots? Would it be some tattooed skinhead a dozen points shy of a GED?"

"Please? Please? Please!"

"Or some sullen, once eager-to-please, dimwit who just steptoes through life like every other dim-sum set-upon slob? Or some strudel-baking sweet grandmama who knits clickingly through every endless Morning Joe?"

The women rolled their eyes and, as soon as it was opportune, nudged themselves with the girl out of the kitchen and out of the house leaving the men and the breakfast remains to deal with each other.

With the women and girl long gone into their tense contentment and the kitchen door closed tightly behind them, Avram Ider muttered something into a splotch of yolk not so easily wiped from the pleather tablecloth.

Then to the forsaken backpack, he intoned his warning, "Watch out for NAZIs, whydontcha?"

*

Three

Holy Smoke

SOMETIMES Carol Ann feels bad because I read that Children's Bible her father bought for her when she was my age.

Dadgantuan flipped it through and said I must just like the pictures. He said he liked 'em too and wanted some to put under his pillow. Carol Ann took it away from him.

Carol Ann told him I ask questions about catholics and saints and angels and martyrs and crusaders and indulgences and Pentecosts. And Nuncoo Stash said she's trying to make a mackerel snapper out of me. She gave him a fun punch then, but her face turned red. I want epiphanies, not stigmatas.

Daddoo said he didn't care what religion I joined as long as I didn't take it too seriously like Anty Smeelia. Then he said his ham sandwich was so good it couldn't be kosher. Stanizeus said that I'd be a hairy tickle in any sex, but Carol Ann said that was "Not Funny!"

I said the new pope was very good and very cute. And everybody said he was better than the last bunch, especially the one who was a NAZI. Dadzuka told Carol Ann I should read whatever I wanted, but some stuff read much more betterer behind closed doors. Carol Ann gave him a fun punch and shook her head so I gave him a fun punch too. And then I gave him a harder one! But not as hard as I woulda if Carol Ann weren't watching.

Stanstoop sang a song about the HMC *Sinsumore and* HMC *stands for Holy Mudder Church. Everybody laughed and I laughed too but all I remember is the part that goes: "No Never? No Never! No Never? Well, hardly ever."*

Zlottie said I'm like C-Moon Vey, but Daddoo said her name was C-Men Vile. He made me sing the song with him, but I like that song tons anyway, and not just because it's by Paul McCartney. Zlottie said Simone Weil would be a saint now if she weren't Jewish. Daddoo said she was mostly a nuisance, especially in Spain where she burnt herself with water like a kucking flutz. He said she even died a nuisance cuz she used a bed could've went to a soldier, but Zottie said she was a SPIRITUAL HERO and didn't want to talk about it anymore with him but she would with me if I want.

I want.

Dadkook said that he would make the best pope ever, and if he couldn't get the good smoke then Stan should try. I know what that means because when they make a new pope, holy white smoke comes out the chimney. But my big papa can't be a pope because he's Jewish and turtle popes don't count.

Anyway, Dadoo Schmoodoo says Anty Schmelia wants us to do some Jewdoo at Obby's grave and we should all go to Obby's Memory Center too. He says cleaning Obby's house is worse than slow spinach torture, but Unco Stooge might come too, so that makes it betterer.

Since we're doing that Boston march, I'm gonna be in a bunch of houses a bunch of times in one week. I dunno how you're supposed to know if somebody's your friend. I guess Jesse's alright. We went to different schools together after being in the same one, and now we both don't go to any.

Fat Jesse REALLY doesn't wanna walk in any march except she doesn't want to say Black Lives don't matter—even though she SERIOUSLY thinks she might kill her parents who are both Black someday. I like being in all kinds of different houses except ours. They're emptier and even more haunted than Obby's. Actually,

Obby's house isn't really haunted at all. My Obby is dead and gone and his house is just as sad as any other place I can go.

Dabba isn't happy any place now. Sometimes when he drops me off here at Stan and Carol's, I think he'd like to just stay too, but Carol Ann can only put up with so much.

*

Four

Squirrel with Pearl Earring

"Now remember when you draw this, I want you should put the house in front of a huge barn seven times grander than the size of their house."

"Why, Obby?"

"Because their barn is stuffed full of stuff from when they were young, from when their children were young, from when their parents were young, from when their grandparents were young. Stuff should be poking out from the barn's broken windows even though their house looks so tidy and nice. From the outside. Do you understand?"

"Yup. Ok. Go ahead, Obby."

Squirrel with Pearl Earring

Walter and Hazel were a lovely old couple who lived in a lovely old house. They loved to sit and swing on their lovely front porch and look lovingly into each other's loving eyes.

"Walter and Hazel? Their last name should be Nutz! Then they could be a pair of swinging nuts!"

"You shut up now, Daddu! Go head now, Obby."

But as much as they loved their house, so did the squirrels.

"I fear these squirrels are eating our house, my dear."

Oh dear! Oh deer! Oh dear!

"What should we do, my dear?"

"My dear, the squirrels must need to eat. So we must feed the squirrels, my dear!"

So Walter bought boxes and bags and sacks and cartons of seeds. Pumpernickel seeds. Sunflower seeds. Caraway seeds. Poppy seeds. Sesame seeds and beseme mucho seeds. Hemp seeds and verklempt *seeds. Chia seeds. Flax seeds. Cucumber seeds. To-mato seeds. Lettuce seeds and salad seeds. Hex seeds. Sex seeds. Mexican jumping seeds. Arizona hump-ing seeds. Even Lotus seeds, Scotus seeds, Potus seeds, and all types of assorted nuts, bolts, knobs, and job seeds.*

"We don't need that Obby. Don't let Daddu help with your stories anymore, ok?"

"Well, but you should still draw lots of acorns and chestnuts. Don't squirrels like those?"

"Where should we put all these seeds, my dear?"
"Yes! Where, my dear? We CAN'T put them in the house!"
"Well, my dear, then I know what we must do. We must clean out the barn!"

CLEAN OUT THE BARN!

In the large barn were heaps of boxes, crates, files, and baskets, piled and stacked in crazy arrangements. Walter and Hazel had to sort through them all.

From the barn they pulled out chairs and posters, pots and potties, lamp-posts and bedsprings, hitching posts and whipping posts, slim candlesticks and fat sticks of kid dynamite.

They pushed out cartons of postcards, boxes of letters, and crumbling old satchels of bills, agreements, proclama-tions, warrants, and deeds.

When large Abe Ider fidgeted, the couch shook beneath the three: the tiny girl, the frail old man, and lard lump Abe. When he finally spoke, the room echoed with morose thunder...

> "They drew out old bills: utility bills, dr. bills, lawyer's bills, bills of attainder, bills of particulars, bills of lading, bills of fare, puffin bills, ostrich beaks, rhino horns, bills of sale, bills past due, bills paid in full, bills never opened in yellowing envelopes with crinkled cellophane windows clouding out demolished addresses of bankrupt firms."

"Stop, Please, Daddu."

> "They uncovered deeds to real estate, commercial, residential, undeveloped and speculative. They undusted titles to aircraft, watercraft, livestock, rolling stock, laughing stock, summer stock, stock it to me, misdeeds, indeeds, deeds of daring du, deeds of daring dead, deeds I do, and deeds I don't, deeds and feats don't fail me now!"

"No Daddu! I mean it! This is not fun now. I don't like this."

"They extricated agreements and contracts, some signed and sealed, some half drafted, some unspoken, forgotten until lit upon and then reconsigned to fitful oblivion."

Sad eyes staring straight ahead, old Abe droned on...

"There were tits for tats, and whacks on rats, and spits for spats, IOUs and you own, me use. And unrequited overtures, misunderstandings gussied up with flimsy language to be documented and waved before ashen, aggrieved, and insulated faces."

"Daddu, pweese! I only wants the regular stories!"

"They rediscovered lost minutes and meeting notes, misdirected and unsent mail, calendars with gaping gaps, sub-poenas, enjoinders, entreaties, false diagnoses, overoptimistic prognoses, prescriptions, prospectives, decisions, ultimatums, confessions, rejoinders, affidavits, memories of questionable evidence: corroborating and exculpatory, actionable and moot."

"Daddy! Daddu! Daddu! Daddu!
You're baddy baddu baddu baddu!
You make me maddy maddu and real mad too!
Why'd my Abba Obby Obbu hafta havya have you?
He musta hadda haddu HAD to.
Stop! NOW!

To cuddle it, she reached down for her knapsack stuffed tightly between her sneakered feet and the sofa's fringe, making sure to scrape, stab, press, and slap her groaning fat dad as brusquely possible while pulling it towards her.

It's ok, Nobby. Go ahead now."

Sobbing, she pushed her grandfather's shaky hand away from her tears as her fat dad slumped back into himself again.

They dragged out napkins and baby clothes, light bulbs and feather fans, bicycles and fencing swords.

They rolled out fishing rods and radios, hampers and hamster cages, harnesses and riding crops.

They lifted out hats half-eaten by moths, lace well

yellowed with age, books dark dusted with mold, and teacups chock filled with moss.

They wheeled out shovels and knives, muskets and cannonballs, cherry bombs, and gas masks. They trundled out cracked mannequins, unstuffed plush-toys, bare-breasted Barbies, headless babydolls, and bodiless troll heads. And they carried out paintings in frames, prints folded in fours, canvases rolled into rolls, and sketches and doodles and engravings in glass. Picture after picture after picture they stacked in the yard.

And they filled up the barn with barrels and casks and cartons of seeds!

"And the squirrels have to help!"

"Yes, my smart girl. Make sure you draw plenty of helpful little squirrels."

Oh, my dear! Now our yard is such a mess!

"Oh my! Yes! There is so much junk and so much stuff and so many treasures and so many things!"

"What shall we do? What shall we do?"

"'I know! I know! We should have a large yard sale! It will be a large Barnyard Bazaar and Everything Must Go!"

LARGE YARD SALE
at
WALTER and HAZEL's

BARNYARD BAZAAR
EVERYTHING *MUST* GO!

And the people came! They came to buy shoes. They came to buy hammocks. They came to buy daintily painted dishes and silvery stirring spoons.

They bought teapots. They bought plastic flowers wire arranged in wine bottles. They bought wind chimes and phonograph platters.

They bought canisters and gas masks. They bought pup tents and compasses. They bought rusty jack knives and broken boomerangs.

They bought wax paper and crayons. They bought coat trees and raincoats. They bought rabbits' feet and cigar boxes of dried-up recipes.

They bought bundles of barbed wire, packages of paraffin, and jam jars of rat poison.

But they didn't buy the sewing machine.

And they didn't buy the paintings.

"Oh dear! Oh dear! What should we do? We CAN'T throw them on the fire!"

Mr. Fixit rubbed his whiskers. Ms. Spinster put her hands on her hips.

"Hazel and Walter! You have the solution to all our problems!"

Mr. Fixit and Ms. Spinster got busy. With Mr. Fixit's pickup, they towed their wooden frame ship with its colorful painting sails to the nearest ocean beach.

And all together they sailed into the bliss of the wide-open seas.

"Don't they go on to Monkey Island, Obby?"

"That's a different story, babyface."

*

Five

Streamly Gredible

"Was my mud always pretty?"

"Your mudder was always a stunner."

"But she was lots more prettier when she was younger. Right?"

"You seen pictures when she was your age. Very cutiepie. Very prettysly. But she grew up and got ever more fetching gorgeous. Didn't she?"

"And then she got even older."

"And I did too."

"You got ugly."

"I was always ugly."

"You got uglier."

"Your mama didn't."

"No. She got less prettier."

"You think so? I don't."

"It was cuz of me."

"No. Even that depression thing. That wasn't cuz of you. It wasn't cuz of any baby. She was always up and down and all around when she wasn't dumped in the downs. She was a live wire blowin fuses, your agitatin' mudder wuz."

"A shocker?"

"A jolter and a zapper and a paddywhack snapper."

"She would've been happier if I never came."

"No. Happy is a crazy thing. Was Obby happy?"

"Sometime he was sad happy. Mudd could be crazy happy sometime. Streamly crazy happy. Or streamly sad crazy."

"OK. Happy's complicated. Sad is streamly complicated. Crazy's crazy complicated. You can't believe books and movies or talking heads. The Nintertubz doesn't know nothing from happy. Your mudder tried to do great things. She was a fighter. An arguer. A challenger. A complainer. An interrogator. A rager changer. She knew things could be better. She did her best. And you were the best thing that ever happened to her."

Greta pulled her knapsack toward her and rested it on her lap.

"I'll never get to make her happy."

*

Six

Downtown Entropy

Hurry up, FatDad! I'm hungry!"

"Hold up, Skinny Imp!"

"How ya going to do this march if ya can hardly move like that?"

With hooded eyes, chubby Jesse and impish Grettie watched as Fat Dad Abe Ider, sweating heavily and wheezing, ceased waddling and threw his arms into the sky.

"The Big Bang is entropy!" he bellowed. "We are the Big Bang!"

"I wanna falafel."

"We are entropy! Entropy is the Chelonian force! We are the Big Bang!

"I wanna falafel!"

"The Big Bang is us. The Big Bang is you," he explained carefully as if to quietly reassure his child everything would somehow be alright. "You too," he said placatingly to Jesse.

"Daddu. I. Just. Want. A. Fucking falafel!"

"But we can't get one now? We'll eat when we're all together? How many meals we gotta eat in one day? Where would we ducking go anyway?"

The girl, her small fingers a tight fist but for index barrel and upthrust thumb, slowly and deliberately raised aim toward her target, the fleshy bridge of her glum pappy's nose. Squinting, with one arm firmly support-ing the other, she snapped the hammer thumb thrice and then glared defiantly up into Abe's widening eyes before sternly glaring straight ahead.

Fat Daddy followed her gaze to the storefront on the near corner.

Falafally Yours

"Ok. But you are entropy too."

*

Seven

A Parable of Peppers

Abe did his very best. I don't care what anyone else says.

It was after the big long march and a somewhat rushed late lunch. Now we were trudging tired through what may once have been the combat zone when my Carrie Ann stopped us short.

Primly, she held it forward like a parole officer might hold a specimen just surrendered by a sketchy suspect soon to be cuffed and sent back to stir in the sheriff's van before all tests had been completed and verified.

"We have a problem," repeated my long-suffering lady, now directing her regard of impatient disappointment and resigned superiority towards Abey–and then again back at me.

"Looks like a jar of tiny green kidneys," I offered weakly.

"Not funny," she said, dismissing me before training her hard glare at poor old Abe.

"It's a jar of peppers," she told him as if that would foreclose the case and convict the pickles.

The five of us stared back as if we all, somehow, were guilty of something.

"From the restaurant," she said, adding another unnecessary detail. And then she frowned at Grettible who smirked a smirk that was almost winsome.

"It has to go back," Care continued. "You two," meaning me and Abey, "have to take both of them back. Zlottie and I will wait across the street."

Zlottie carefully walked over to her side, turning righteously against the rest of us.

Across the street was the Common and the Red Line

which could take us back to Alewife. And the T was a somewhere where we might sit down.

On the other hand, I was curious to walk back, my gaze uncensored–as if it might be possible to recognize anything so sordid so long gone in a place visited so infrequently for such very short times so long ago. Now the only semi-tempting attraction was a store selling ecclesiastical robes. There was at least one bishop getup in the display window, but perhaps a slim possibility we could buy a papal vestment there too. Maybe. And Gretzel seemed so serious about dressing like an altar boy, Carol said she might sew her something. "It would be easy and cheap if nothing had to be pleated."

A pope suit would not be cheap. It would actually be quite comical on Abey, but the amount of material required to drape him would make such a thing especially exorbitant. Still, he was sorely tempted, enamored with the idea of being a jowly Jewish pope. And that bastard, after all, could afford it.

Abe called her "Scary Carey." If she were a little thinner and less pretty, she could more pervasively convey the air of a New England spinster in the Margaret Hamilton mode. But if she were boney I'd just have to buy her an umbrella with a parrot head and a Mary Poppins coat and hat. Not that she'd wear it. "Not Funny!" she'd say.

At this point, we were all shifting uncomfortably

on tired feet–even Zlottie who had been granted a dispensation.

Later it became clear Jessie was the rat who shyly shoved the jar under Carrie's nose, but Grettie never held it against her as far as I know. As far as I know, The Gret was quite satisfied with how everything turned out. For one thing, the little Git was always different around Carrie Anne. The two have some kind of understanding which works out fairly well for everyone. The little girl and her fat dad were too intense to be together all the time, and having the kid around–as troubled as she was and even if it were sometimes more than a week at a time–still seemed like almost nice vacations for all of us.

I'll never stop saying that Abe always did the best he possibly could.

Now on this particular day in the city, little Gretzie was still quite spritely on her mean little feets. Poor plump Jesse though was clearly fading so the extra steps would be quite a penance. But with my bad knees groaning over my sore feet, I was the one true victim there, even though Abey would probably suffer the most, what with already dragging his weight around, and him literally limping through the whole long and winding march through Bostontown.

He really did do his best, you know.

Abe was a powerful and persistent man. And now

it was his kid who, once again, had insulted propriety and (Mark D. Chapmanlike) offended all. So we schlepped back, all four of us toward the Place of Pho. We returned the jar to its original table and, demurely, the girls apologized to a dumbly astounded waiter. Well, Jessie seemed truly penitent, but Gretel was clearly overacting, the idea of "penance" to her being quite exotic, romantic, and (who knows?) maybe somewhat incipiently venereal.

And poor old Abey, who really did mostly do the best he could, might have made a damn good pope too—except for being a Jewish atheist pagan turtle worshiper, I mean.

The Black Lives Matter walkathon had been Zlottie's idea. Carol Anne was immediately all in, so that meant so was Grendel, and that meant me and Abe were roped in as well. Jessie's parents had other commitments, but I have to wonder about them. They didn't know me. They didn't know my Carol Anne. They couldn't have known Zlottie very well either since none of us really did. Even Able didn't, though he'd confided they were already considering whether they might ask Gredible if she could move in for a while.

But Jesse's parents? I mean who'd entrust their only child to someone like Avram Ider even for a short round of miniature golf, never mind his dizzyingly fast drives into the city hub for a march that could turn violent for all anyone knew?

But maybe they got some warm feeling from Abe? For all his superficial lack of wholesomeness, he was the soul of decency. And since we all lived in lily-white Volvo-driving towns, it might be good for the two girls to experience an urban scene and a diversity of Social Justice Warriors of all stripes and colors.

And despite snotnose marshals officiously enforcing rectitudes of political correction, and despite double blue ribbons of polite bike police inexorably corralling us into a cloverleaf-covered cul-de-sac, and despite overzealous lesbians chanting "This is what democracy looks like!," it was, except for its toll on aching legs, a nearly pleasant experience. The kids stayed engaged, and surely this was one incarnation of an essential aspect of democracy?

And pepperless we limped back, stepping down into a tunnel, allowing a tube to trundle us (somewhat restfully) part of our ways home.

* * *

Stan says Avram only did his best. I can't accept that.

A man like Avram had no business bringing up a child, especially not a *girl*. The best he could? He had no filter.

Adulting means having a filter especially when it comes to children. After all, it's up to *us* to protect them–sometimes from ourselves.

Having the girl for weeks or months was like a *vacation?* Well for Stan, maybe.

I *swear* Stanley can be even more irresponsible than Avram ever was. It's a good thing Stan and I never had children. A good thing.

And it's like they suck the life out of me. But what can I do? A motherless child? We have to all pitch in, don't we? But why do I end up doing all the work while everyone else only has fun and games? And some people... They *think* they're being funny? Some things *just* aren't. And some people are not as funny as they may think they are!

But she cries, you know. Stanley doesn't see it. Some people only see what they want. She wouldn't let Avram see her sob probably because she sensed he couldn't take it. He couldn't handle it. A big goofy man like that! I always stopped her when she'd smack or kick her dad, but part of me always wanted to pile on. Still do. And that's it. That's just *it*.

*

Eight

Life is NOT all Carrots and Cream

Rhonda Rabbit had three ears.

That meant she was different, and rabbits are timid creatures. They go hippity hoppity, hippity hoppity from one hiding place to another. New things upset them and make them go hoppity hippity away to hide.

Rhonda Rabbit had three ears.

So Rhonda Rabbit found a hole and made it deeper and bigger and safer, and clever.

But first, she made stone swinging doors to shut so badgers, stoats, ferrets, and weasels could never get in.

Then she made all types of hidey places for carrots and strawberries, turnips and truffles, onions and rhubarb stalks.

These places were all very deep down so it was never too cold and never too hot.

And there were places to breathe if floods came.

"That was my idea"

"And a very good idea too. Thank you, sweet girl."

And no fire could burn her. Ever.

And she kept busy carving statues from root-wood to decorate her tunnels and chambers.

And she made wine from berries to make her gay, and brandy from plums to warm her tum-tum.

It was a lovely perfect place for a timid three-eared rabbit. But she was lonely too.

One day while picking dandelions for her soup and for a nice salad of spinach, parsley, and peppercorns, she met Lou the Kangaroo.

They fell in love. And she hoppity hipped and he bounced and gallumped everywhere with her under the bright open sky.

Then they cooled their toes in the wide rushing river.

And he put her in his pouch and together they gallumped here and there, far and wide.

"Boy kangaroos don't have pouches. Only Mudder kangaroos!"

"But Stu is a Mama's boy!"

"No, Obbey. No!"

"OK. So now the kangaroo is LuLu? And what should the rabbit be?"

"I don't know! Papoop! What should the rabbit be?"

"Dunno, Snugg. Howabout Wrascally Wabbit? Howabout BoomBoom the Bunny? Howabout Cassidy

Hop-along? Howabout TickleCrack the Hare?
Howabout Rosencrantz, the Boy Rabbit?"

"Ok. so..."

> But Rosencrantz Rabbit was too big to stay in Lulu's pouch without hurting her. *Ouch!*
>
> And often the poor wittle wabbit got bounced out and onto the rocks. *Ouch! Ouch!*
>
> And there were so many weasels, wolves, foxes, and stoats. So many eagles, hawks, condors, falcons, and vultures.
>
> And farmers don't like it when rabbits or kangaroos pick their raspberries. *Boom. Boom! BOOM! Ratatattat!*
>
> So it was still not easy for Rosencrantz Rabbit to be out in the wild world.
>
> And Lulu Kangaroo was too big for the rabbit hole no matter how big and deep and comfy it was.

> But Lulu could get her nose in, and they could smooch.
>
> Lulu could get her toes in too, and Rosy would paint them pomegranate and puce and a very lovely chartreuse.

"What's puce and what's chartreuse?"

"One's the color of a rotten plum and the other looks like snot dissolved in monkey pee."

"Go away now, Daddoo!"

> But they wanted to be together. Safe. For always.
>
> So one day Lulu Kangaroo gallumped into the village and found a shrewd voodoo handyman.
>
> He rubbed her all over with shortening cream. Especially her big legs. He used special painless pulleys to stretch out her ears.

"*I'm glad you made them painless, Obby.*"

"You have such good ideas because you have such a good heart."

And that very same night Rosencrantz Rabbit crept into the very same village to see the very same handyman.

Hans the Handyman rubbed the special shortening cream onto Rosencrantz's ears and pumped up his legs with Super Olympic Jumping Juice. That juice was so super juicy-good, it made the rest of him bigger too.

Now Lulu was a rabbit who'd be safe and comfy in the wonderful rabbit warren.

And now Rosencrantz was a kangaroo who could bound and jump across fields and over rivers.

Too bad he was too big to squeeze into his old hidey-hole anymore. But he was larger than any hawk or weasel. And too fast for any bear or wolf. Plus, he could punch!

"That's berry important, you know."

"I know, my sweet girl. Thank you for thinking of it."

> **And they could still nuzzle noses at the door of the Rabba-Roo hole.**
>
> **And Rosencrantz learned to love having painted toenails.**

"But they should have talked to each other! And that bad handyman should have said something."

"But aren't stories for children to learn something?"

*

...and the Riverbank Talks

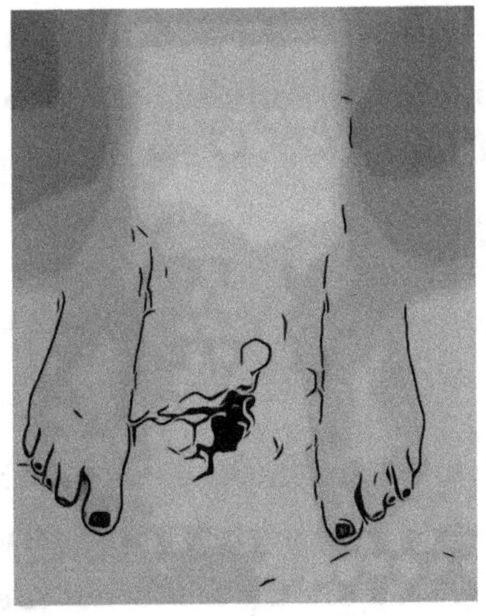

Carol Anne's phone voice was authoritative and reassuring. "So you found them alright?"

"Yup. Yup. CVS. Yup. She's got them and knows just what to do. Just pull the paper thing off and it sticks on the underwear very very nice. She's in the bathroom now. Uh... How long fore she gots to change it for another one?"

"She'll know, but drive her here. How is she?"

"Shaky shaky. And so white it's scary, Carol. I was frightened to leave her, but she wouldn't get in the car. I put a towel and everything. But she's not crying like that anymore. Just very shaky. I wrapped her in a blanket, but she got up and cleaned a lot of it, but there's more I don't think she noticed or she'd of freaked out again."

"You need to get her over here or I won't be able to sleep. Put her on the phone, OK?"

"Yup. Yup. Carol Anne? She knew about this. I mean, this is pretty early unexpected, but she had the books and I know she read them 'cuz of what she sniped about it all."

"It's early, Abe. But not unheard of. Not abnormal at all. Every girl reacts differently and she's... You're doing the best you can, I know. But just let me talk to her."

Abe tapped on the busted door. He waited and knocked again.

"Gretty? Gretty, sweetheart? Open the door, please. Carol Anne's on the phone here forya. There's nothing to worry about, OK? Just open the door. OK? She's worried about you, but everything's ok. OK? She just needs to talk to you!"

He listened with his hand on the doorknob, his hip fitting without contact into the curve it had crushed only minutes before into the ruined door.

"Gretty? Can you open this door, please? Or just tell me to wait? Please? I don't wanna open it by myself. OK? It hurts to break doors down. It's not like the movies, goddamn it. Please Gretty? Please? Pretty please?"

He tried to register the sound of his own voice. Could he be panicking her?

He dropped it down an octave and spoke slowly. "Listen Gretty. Take your time, but Carol Anne just wants to know you're ok. OK? We can be there in two hours. Do you need different clothes? I'll just get them. OK?"

"Listen Gretty." His voice was high again. "I'll go through this door again. You want me to count again?

You want we should go to court again? " He cracked open the cracked door and counted down slowly.

She was huddled, wet-eyed, in the dry tub wrapped in a stained blanket. She took the phone and sobbed softly to Carol's voice, answering in monosyllables.

"*Ok,*" she said so softly, getting slowly up and out. Beneath the blanket, he could see she was dressed in mostly clean clothes. She let him wipe her face. He hoped she thought he wiped only tears, taking pains to ensure she saw none of the blood smeared there and everywhere in her recent frenzy.

"*Ok,*" she sobbed, grabbing the CVS package from the floor and surrendering it to her hulking dad.

"*Ok,*" she said, walking stiffly through the cold mist, dragging her blanket through aching puddles, and climbing wet-eyed into the glistening car.

"*Yes,*" she said into the phone. "*Ok. I know... I know.*"

"*Ok,*" she said, "Yes...*Yes. Yes.*"

And the windshield wipers slapped and thumped, thumped and slapped.

And that's how she was driven through the March

darkness until the end of strain somewhere on the beat of the lonesome road before they splashed through Leominster where the phone slipped silently out of her sleeping hand.

"A cliff. A fall. Nothing at all."

*

Ten

Extra Dimensions

"You're not worried she's not in school?"

"Hey, Stan... What the frig can I do? If I drag her kicking and biting through the front door, she runs out the back. If I drop her little butt in the office, she bolts the first opportunity. You know how many times she flushed her batteries? And what happens if she hurts someone there? She's already in Special Ed which is a big freak'n mortification as far as she concerns."

"I like tads fine. Jest don't wanna be widdem all day."

"They're not retads, you little spurt. There's lots of very 'telligent morons in that class."

"They are fuffups".

"Well, who the frig's not a freak'n fuggup? ...Me? Stan? You, ya little cumdrop?"

Cooly, Streamly Gredible sashayed into the next room, but not before bending forward, thrusting a stiff middle finger sharply into the air, and shaking its fist at her blubbery dad.

"...See what I mean? ...She'll say stuff to hurt other kids' feelings just so they'll kicker out. A lotta them have shit self-esteem already. But she's not above lobbing blunt objects. How many posters do I gotta tape over holes in the walls back home? I don't want her–or me–involved in that kind of stuff anymore. Keeps me up at night. And then ever morn I gotta drag her outta bed? Anyway, she's doing alright with Maths and Catholicism."

"Sorry about that."

"Why? She's damned well-behaved with Carol Anne. And there's lots of history and drama there. The other night she proclaimed herself the *Ummacculate Receptacle* which is about as good a malaproptender as I've heard. Pretty soon she'll challenge me to play *Name dat Pope*."

"Receptacle? You think she meant it that way?"

"Wadda I know? I'm jest try'n to keep my chin above watta here. I don't understand what's going on. I mean, this is all way outta boundage–even considering. We don't know who we are, what we are."

"Abe, you think it's true you can't understand reality without Math?"

"Stan, you can't DO PHYSICS without Maths, but equations ultimately don't help you understand any-thing. Maths don't describe nuttin any betterer than your eyes, your nose, or your ears can describe sumpin. You *sense* a thing in all kinds of ways, but that doesn't let ya describe it. Try describing music. You can't. Like our udder senses, Maths are just ways to detect what might be out there and what it might be doing. But like other sense organs, Maths can be deceived, or help us deceive ourselves. Feynman said if we lost all our Maths, Physics would be set back by about one week."

"Are you joking, Mr. Iderer? So it don't describe nothing, just predicts or detects stuff? Tell me something new and interesting."

"I dunno. Some LHC data indicates there's at least four other dimensions needed to understand ...describe what's going on."

"Eight dimensions? How do they get at that?"

"You're axing me? Surely you're joking, Mr. Immie! But imagine a 3-D geodesic globe. A lattice of interlocking hexagons. Now picture its shadow on a flat surface. Our senses are so limited, that's all they can grab! How long does it take us to realize this sense impression is jest a projection of some globular crystal when we can only see in two dimensionals? And what if that glob's rotatin' and wobblin' with multiple protrusions sticking out–and other structures whizzing by at crazy odd intervals?"

"Like Plato's cave, eh?"

Well, ...er, our senses can only grab what data they

were devolved to grasp. We're simply not quipped to gasp those udder dimensions. So only limited data gets fed to the Caligulas in our brains. But Maths extends what devolution quipped us with for caligulating what we needed to figure out in the bushes to hunt and gatherate... Ah, fuggit. Let's see if we can connive that kid into eating sumpin halfway nutritional."

"Shut up and masticate?"

"Yeah. And swallow and keep it down."

*

Eleven

A Box in a Box

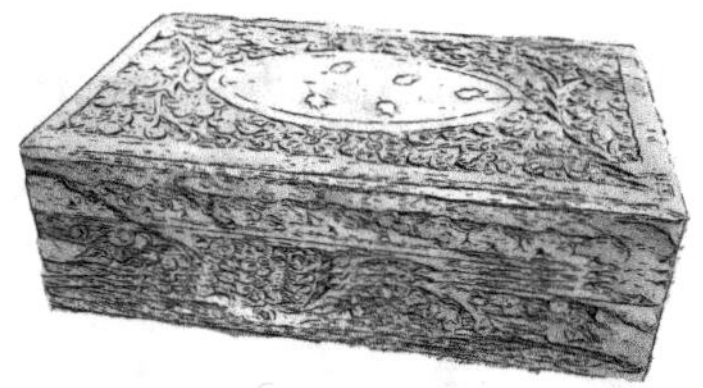

"I'm a little cumdrop, snort and shout."

"Gadzamighty! Please?"

"Roll me over. Spit me out."

"Nice. Very nice. I'm sorry. Ok?"

"Wanna do music?"

"Ok, Baby. Let's do music!"

"Ok, Baddad. My list first." She checked the connections.

"Please don't call me that. D'ya think you could please take that offya first?"

"Ok," she chirped and shimmied out of the knapsack. She set it carefully on the side table, almost under his nose.

Hers came on loud, but she turned it louder and began to move. With regard to neither tempo nor beat, she stepped and hopped and wriggled and swayed. Her YouTubed moves included approximations of frugs and shimmies, disco poses, and sly signs from hip-hop.

Mournfully he watched the eternal antics of childhood phasing backward and forward from times to timelessness, from naive fluency to clumsy estimations of nubility. Then, quickly responding to a warning glare, he pushed himself up and launched into his signature Russian duckwalk.

Intentionally ignoring the music, he began to awkwardly whirl and hop. He dosey'd and doe'd, unsynching his paces and carroting his toes. He cakewalked and contorted, bouncing almost gracefully on one foot. Then, floor shaking, he'd jump into flying pirouettes with stumbling landings extending into dangerous wobbles and abrupt twists, concluding with "*A Cha Cha*"s in Jimmy Durante rasps and minstrelsy hand flutters.

Gasping with mirth, she screamed and giggled as he, again and again, almost, but did not fall. Inevitably, commanded by weakening knees, he slowed into a series of sad stances and silly shuffles so she could selfwrap into her own slow whirls, soft steps, and shifting reveries he fretted could never be as sweet as he so helplessly hoped. And, cautiously with but one eye at a time, he'd try to watch her as if there were some singular way to observe without disturbing while, just as carefully, she'd constantly reassure herself his attention was there but not overbearing.

After a while, he'd make his way back to his chair and pretend to sleep. When her list finally played out, she'd gently pretend to wake him. And as she perched on his lap his music would already be playing.

This night, collapsed in his favorite armchair with her head on his shoulder, he reached out to touch the knapsack lightly with one finger.

"Scary Carey says you found a nice box for the nice box."

Digging sharp knees into his soft thigh, she reached over and unzipped. Pulling out a velvet sack, purple as dark prose, she undid the drawstrings and, soft-eyed, she handed it to him.

"It's lovely. Very lovely. We are so lucky to have Carol Ann."

"And Nunco Stashu too."

"And Nuncle Stosh too. Isn't it heavy to carry around?"

"Carie Annie put soft strips in the knappy. And quilty stuff." **She showed him the inside of her knapsack.** *"The cushystrips are underneath."*

"Oh, that Carey is so scary. This is just wonerfill, wonerful. So, it's comfy to carry?"

"Very."

She ran her hands over the box that contained a box and, with a crumpled frown, she toyed with its clasp. She pushed it slowly back into the plush bag, pulling the drawstrings tight. Then, carefully, she replaced the whole hardsoft package into her childish backpack and zipped it closed securely.

"You know you don't have to go with us down to Abba's. Right? When Stan and me leave, you can stay with Scary Carrie. She says it's alright."

"I wanna go with you and Stosh to Obby's."

"That means the unveiling and everything. Don't you wanna stay with Carol Anne?"

"Yeah. But I wanna go with you two."

"I'm sorry, you know."

"For what, Snafu?"

"For everything sweetcheeks. For everything."

"Everything is not up to you. Everything is not your fault."

"I know. But I'm still very sorry."

"Well, you better stop, or I'll go off."

"Don't go off tonight. Ok?"

"I won't Daddy. I won't." She rested her head again and sighed like a tired infant.

His music played on.

A Love Supreme

*

Part II

House of Quips

Are We There Yet?

Are we there yet?"

"Bubala! Bubala!" pleaded odd Abe in his best old Jew whine, "Furcrissakes we just got on the furshiltin' freeway! We'll get to Obby's this morning, Ok? That's if the traffic's not too crazy."

"We should have real GPS. Then I wouldn't have to ax you."

Tense driven Abe sped up, pushing and pushed to get to a place he did not want to go. "Doesn't your thingy play movies? Why dontcha watch *Donnie Darko* again?"

"No. I want Nuncoo Stoshoo to tell a story."

"Ok. Which one?"

"Anything but the Snotlaws again, Stanman. It gave me a headache in my tuchus last night."

"Snotlaws! That's what I want. Go Stashu go!"

"Give the pinheads what they want. Right, Abey?"

"For fugs sake..."

"Hurry up! When your pappy was a boy..."

"Ok. When my papa was a boy, his papa needed a safe place to stow him once in a little while and from time to time."

"Why? Why? Why?"

"Well, sometimes his papa needed to go to Wyoming and be a cowboy. Other times he needed to travel light and keep outta sight and go real deep into Elvis country."

"There was no Elvis then! Elvis weren't even bored yet."

"Well, it wasn't called Elvis country back then, but was even more Gothic."

"What's Gothic?"

"That's where people keep their dogs under the porch all year and marry a new first cousin every spring. Anyway, my papa's papa dropped my papa off on Snotlaw Mountain up in the Catskills where he'd be safe."

"Why was that place so safe? It was a horrible place!"

"Well, Daddy Snotlaw, Grandpa SnotLaw, Gramma Snotlaw, and all the Snotlaw boys with their uncles and cousins had rifles and shotguns and could kill goats with their minds."

"Why?"

"Why? Well to protect their stills of course. They also had a coal mine where they worked their Hebrew slaves. They sold illegal electricity until Simon D. Roysenfelter put them outta business with the TBA. They also had a workshop that made silent duck callers, rubbers, French Ticklers, and a printing press for ten-dollar bills and French postcards."

"What's French Postcards?"

"They're regular postcards with dirty jokes written in French and sometimes naked ladies."

"What are rubbers and French ticklers?"

"Rubbers go over your shoes to keep them dry when it rains, and French Ticklers are like little feather dust- ers so boys can tickle their girlfriends."

"What's the big deal with that?"

"Well, it's the same as with the moonshine whiskey they stilled. The Snotlaws wouldn't never pay any sales tax. And it was Prohibition back then, so prac- tically everything except church on Sundays was prohibited."

"So the revenuers was always trying to climb Snotlaw Mountain?"

"Right. But they didn't have any more chance than a lost hobo. The Snotlaws were all crack shots. They had Tommy guns and a Gatlin gun too just in case. The Hatfields and the McCoys were there too. So was the Ku Klux Kan. Ya couldn't get away with that now because the Feds have airplanes and helicoopters and cruise missiles and drones now. But this was the twenties."

"Why didn't they use big artillery cannons? They had those in World War I."

"Hmm... good question. Snotlaw Mountain was too high, I guess. And anyway there's the Posse Commies-notus law which was much more strictly enforced back them days when America was great."

"And those Snotlaws was very tough. Right?"

"Are you kidding? And mean too. One time some low-life Irish Mafia types started a gang war by stiffing them in a hooch deal. So the Snotlaws, Deputy Barney Fife, and High Sheriff Andy Gritshole all get in their big old Snotlaw jalopy and drive to Beverly Hills and kidnap Al Capone and drug him back to their pigpen and mack him bark like a dog."

"Cool. Whatabout poor MaryEllen? And, Dabba stop groaning, or I'll make him tell it again! And stop fartin too!

"Then you stop snortin!"

"Never mind him, Stanzu. Jest keep goin."

"Ok. So poor MaryEllen would get knocked up every year, and they never know'd who done it until the baby was born. If it had a hairlip, it was JohnBoy's. If it had red hair, it was Jimmygabob's. If it had grey hair, it was Granpa Snotlaw's. If it had six toes, it was Pa's. If it had a dark complexion, it was Sammy Dave's. If it was retarded, it was Gilligan's. If it came out circumcised, it was Yehudi Bitumen's. If it was a boy who dressed like a girl, it was Klinger Jim's. If it liked matzoh balls, it was Dustin Portnoy's. If it was very smart, it was the Professor's who kept inventing new brews for the Snotlaws to sell and had a weakness for pigtailed farm girls."

"What if it sung good?"

"If it sang good, it was either Sherman Bobby's or Cassidy Dave's. If it had pointy ears, it was old Doc Schlock's, the town teethpuller who did abortions on the side."

"But then they got on TV."

"It wasn't them. First, somebody wrote a sappy story getting the Snotlaws all backwards and made them look like scrappy hillbillies trying to survive during the Depression. But by the time the Depression hit, the real Snotlaws had all moved west and opened the first casino in Sinsity, Utah. Then Bugsy Seigelmen, Hymen Roth, and the Sicilian Godfathers came and wiped them all out on Saint Valentine's Day."

"And that was so sad, right?"

"So sad. They even got Jimmy GumBob. That always made my father very sad. Every Valentine's Day my old pappy would drink to his memory, and he'd always groan, "Poor little Jim Bob. Poor little cock-sucker. Poor little bug-eyed bastard!"

"Cool. Are we there yet?"

"Howbout you put your seatbelt across your mout?"

"Papoopy?"

"What shitass?"

"I'm gonna be a boy now."

"That's nice. I'll call a moyle"

"And you gotta call me he."

Abe gunned down on the pedal and passed five cars. "When sheeps fly upside down I will."

"You got to. It's gonna be a law."

"What? If somebody says they're a ficus tree, I gotta offer dem Miracle Grow instead of coffee?"

"It's only polite, you know."

"Fine. We'll keep some in the cabinet."

"Daddy?"

"**What now?**"

"Are we there yet?"

*

Thirteen

Under Water

...save his ashes too. Obby's house right here was just fine, but it's still way too close to where the flood was then. They want me to sleep in Antsy Schmilia's room upstairs, but I won't. Her grownup house got diloojed. She had to move in with us for a month. She brought her own food. And new pots and pans only she could use.

She didn't drown. But lots of cats and dogs? So probably squirrels and chipmunks too. And rabbits. Nobody tried to save them. That's wrong. So wrong. And what about the foxies Carol Ann feeds with peanuts, NOT granola, in her garbage pile? What if North Hamster got flooded too? Fat Poopoo always sings 'bout 'em...

Wander what the foxies are doing tonight!~
Wander what the foxies are doing tonight?

I always wander too, especially when it rains and snows. They're good foxies when they're not bad foxies who eat the poor wittle meeses, but the bad widdle meeses eat their own baby mooses too and that's natch. I wonder if Sticky and Minnie Moose make cartoon babies just to eat them?

Stan and Carol have two different houses. Me and Poops have three. And some people don't have any. Obby only had this one. I don't know how many Zeyde Z has, and blessed means wounded in France. Poops says none of them are really house homes. The one I know isn't, but once you go up the elevator and get inside, it's kinda like a house with somebody who cooks for you anything you want, even octopus with soy mustard sauce which turned out to be pretty tasty good. But Obby had that too except she only cooked Polish food and normal stuff when it was mealtimes.

Uncouth Numskull Stanush says Meekie is a racist troop 'cuz he wears white gloves like the White Irish who dressed like that to make fun of Blacks for being jimcrows. But I don't like Meekie Moose like I do Screwy Jewloose back in the day when he was a kidnik and Deeno Marvelous had to take care of him even though he was a mean little snot brat like me.

Screwy is too scream funny so I can't breathe, but Deeno was too, and both was fenzy good zinger boys. But in the movies, Deeno did all the REAL singing so dumb kids like my Fat Dad could go buy popcorn and sodas and make them a clump of escarole money. Mean ol money man Zeyede Z even knows Screwy Lewis so I could meet him maybe, but Poops says he's too old and mean now and it would make me sadder.

I wish Obby were here still. I can't sleep with just Mr. Schnoob. Daddu won't sleep with us now. And Nunco Stan won't. They won't even let me ax them.

At Carol Ann's, Gracie and Marbles will sleep in a bed with me or on a couch. At least Gracie will. Mommy wouldn't never let me sleep with her. Carol Ann will sleep with me when Stosh isn't home. I like sleeping on the couch where people walk by.

Carey Ann won't ever come with us to dead Obby's. She won't get in a car with Schmoodoo. But he drives real good even though he goes too fast and makes crazy moves. He never gets in an accident and only got a ticket just once. Mommy Mud always got tickets and had lots of accidents even before I was born. I was in two of them but I only remember one. Mr. Schnoob is no good. He doesn't breathe or make noise or move.

Carol Ann is like my Mudd cuz when she says something, she believes it no matter what. But I'm like my Dudd cuz I don't. Stories tear you away from the truth and tear means cut, and tear means cry too and tears are like rain escape they have salt like the soda ocean.

In *Saving Mr. Banks, her mudder's sister came to take care of her Daddoo. She had Mary Poppins' umbrella. I read the book and saw the movie where Mr. Banks had money, but not like Zeyde but more like Obbie. He never drank whiskey, rum, wine, beer, gin, or absinthe and when Mary Poppins popped in, she made everything alright. Real life is not like that.*

Carol says Mr. Schnoob smells like pee and she's right so I will burn him.

*

Fourteen

The Land of Kootsie Boobie

"Obby read me a story."

"Which story, my beautiful girl?"

"The one about the Snakes and The Giant Boulder!"

"That's my favorite too. So..."

The Land of Kootsie Boobie was once a land of happy people.

And that was how it was. Until the time of memory.

Before the time of memory, everyone was busy and happy being busy happily doing what they did best.

Before the time of memory, Al Stupido would roll a giant boulder up Pointy Top Hill because pushing rocks around was his best thing. He would roll the boulder up until it got right to the tipipity top, and then it would roll backwards on its only.

Sometimes he would roll the boulder right over the top, and then it would roll down the far side of the hill. Al Stupido liked a little change now and then.

One day Al Stupido's giant boulder rolled down the hill just the wrong way. It smashed into the house of Enshreiko Croonruso and his lovely daughter Smelia Flowers. Luckily no one was home.

"Is that like real life?

"Shut up you, Daddoo!"

And luckily Enshreiko, who was best at screaming songs, had always wanted to try being a carpenter.

So Enshreiko happily built a beautiful new house, and (when

Smelia told him to) Al Stupido happily rolled another boulder right between it and Pointy Top Hill. Just in case.

Then the lovely Smelia Flowers gave Al Stupido a new idea. Al Stupido was always interested in getting new ideas because he never had any on his own.

Smelia suggested that instead of rolling the giant boulder up Pointy Top Hill so it could roll down again and smash somebody's house, Al Stupido could roll it in a great circle all around the Land of Kootsie Boobie.

The lovely Smelia Flowers measured the feet of Al Stupido. She also weighed the weight of the Giant Boulder and tested Al Stupido's muscle power. She did some arithmetic and calculated that Al Stupido could roll the Giant Boulder around The Land of Kootsie Boobie every three moons and still have a day in between for a regular celebration of his quarterly feat of strength.

The lovely Smelia Flowers was a prodigy at doing arithmetic. She could figure out the day of the week someone was born. She could calculate the phases of the moon, and every year on their birthday she would give everyone in The Land of Kootsie Boobie a copy of her famous calendar.

She could even predict the exact times of day for each sunrise *and sunset which was not very difficult because those things happened pretty much the same time every day.*

The only thing that made it hard was nobody in The Land of Kootsie Boobie had a clock.

And nobody else in The Land of Kootsie Boobie could do arithmetic which meant nobody really knew if Smelia's calculations were correct. Or not.

But something soon started to make the Lovely Smelia Flowers a little less happy. Instead of looking at her famous calendar, the Kootsie Boobieans simply waited for Al Stupido to come around again with his Giant Boulder so everyone could have a happy festival. This was something to look forward to. And to remember.

And then Mr. Moe Moneypays, the exercise instructor and bean counter, had an idea of his own.

What if he wrote down everything that happened in The Land of Kootsie Boobie between each festival which meant between every arrival and every departure of Al Stupido? This was how the Time of Memory began.

And that was when Mr. Moe Moneypays changed his name to Mr. Mo Manydays.

At first, this was just fine with everyone in The Land of Kootise Boobie because nothing much happened there anyways.

And still, everybody was happy doing what they did best. Enshreiko Croonruso nailed boards together. The Lovely Smelia Flowers did arithmetic. Mr. Mo Manydays taught exercises and kept memories. Every night the Kootsie Boobieans would come and listen to Enshreiko Croonruso shriek. And every weekend they would watch Three Fingers Lefty, who ran the sawmill during the week, play baseball all by himself. And that was quite a sight to see.

But rolling the Giant Boulder all around the land was bad for the snakes. The rumbling made them nervous because Rolling Stones made it unsafe for them to lie in the grass. So the snakes played tricks on Al Stupido. They dug big holes so the boulder would fall in, and it took a long time for Al Stupido to push the boulder out again.

The Lovely Semelia Flowers had never figured on that. Neither had Mr. Mo Manydays. So now the calendars looked wrong and there was never any time to have happy rock festivals. Al Stupido never knew if he was coming or going and he could never stop rolling the Giant Boulder.

People had gotten used to keeping track of time by Al Stupido and his Giant Boulder, and there wasn't anybody who really understood how The Lovely Semelia Flowers could make her calendars except Smelia herself. And soon nobody knew whether they were coming or going or just running around in circles.

Now, this might not sound too bad to you because you're probably used to it. But the people of Kootsie Boobie were used to being happy. They were not used to worrying or even thinking. And all of this was very upsetting to them.

And they stayed nervous even though Mr. Mo ManyDays invented bases for baseball to make it seem like running around in circles was something to cheer about.

And the people remained very uneasy even though Enshreiko Croonruso put down his hammer and nails after the baseball game every Saturday and entertained them with electrifying operatic song singing.

Many blamed Al Stupido. Others blamed the snakes. Lots of people blamed the Lovely Smelia Flowers because, after all, she gave the idea to Al Stupido who was much too simple to think for himself.

There were a few people who blamed Enshreiko Croonruso or Three Fingers Lefty, but it was hard to know why. They might have invented reasons to make themselves seem clever, or they may have just imagined them.

But most people blamed Mr. Mo Manydays. Some did this because his writings helped them remember how they used to be happy, and this made them even sadder. Others blamed him because they thought he should have kept some memories away from some people who were much better off forgetting.

Eventually, Mr. Mo Manydays passed away. So did Al Stupido, Enshreiko Croonruso, and Three Fingers Lefty. Snakes never die. They just shed their skins.

The Lovely Semelia Flowers grew very old and gray and bent. Little children were afraid of her. And everyone forgot about the Giant Boulder even though it was always there, covered with moss. But now The Land of Kootsie Boobie was always troubled.

And some people, for some reason, felt it was better not to remember what was long ago in the past. But others, even though they did not know why, believed it was important to never forget.

*

Fifteen

Only Forward

AMAZON RABITTRESS SEEKS PIGMY
KANGAROO FOR HOPPING GOOD TIMES

SQUIRREL WITH PEARL EARRING TAKES
OLDSTER COUPLE ON FINE ARTS SAIL

NEBBISH TAILOR LEARNS PERILS OF SALTY
CUTUPS FROM BAGHDAD BEVY

PLACID ISLANDERS LOSE INNOCENCE BUT
GAIN ANXIETY

WAN WIDOWER YEARNS ENTRY TO ETERNITY
WHILE EVERYONE WAITS

"Boyoboyo boyo! Nobbie sure was a berry busy book writer!"

"Yup, and when your Abba died, Kinko's stock sunk 22 points."

They paused.

A sleek black convertible pulled haltingly up the drive distracting from their tasks. One tire dug heavy into overgrown grass and, blazing, a fender projected obliquely into the street.

Both stood staring.

Gretchen Sarah Ider raised soft eyes to catch the wide ones of Stanislaus Anthony Imerese. Purposefully, she trotted from the open garage toward the ancient driver with Stan starting a slow ten paces behind.

A large boney palm with ring-weighted fingers beckoned her to hurry. They coiled and unfurled imperiously, protruding from a watchband of gold glowing brighter than the gauzy morning sunlight. The owner caught Stan gazing at blue-black numbers starkly visible beneath their arm's hair, heavy straight and dark. A quick eyebrow arch, more amused than challenging, jerked Stan Imerese to shift quickly back and away.

"Come here so I see you better." The dark papyrus hand cupped her chin, lifting her face for its man's satisfaction. *"Every time you grow more into your beauty. Do you know that? Do you study and learn? Does fat papa keep you busy at books? Books keep lovely girls from troubles. Do you know? He should know."*

He surveyed her calmly. An upturned palm extended a silent invitation for her to grasp it, and she cautiously complied. *"He inside?"* He shrugged toward the doomed house with his chin.

"He's boxing and sorting more," she explained in sad resignation.

"Hmph. Go tellem I'm here. Right?"

Gretel loped quickly into the house.

"So you helping Avram. You his friend." The same shrug. *"Any timetable yet? He wait for market to bounce back?"* The old man shook his head, pleasurably dismayed at the world's inextinguishable folly.

Another man, younger but shrunken in limp squatness, sat forward facing and impassive beside him. *"Meet my son, Benny. Benny! Say hello to the friend of Avram!"*

Benny turned a childish smile. His thin voice

squeaked, "Hi, pleased to meetchew. My name is Benny," and Benny, once his greeting was requited, turned again silently forward.

"This my son, Benny." Now the old man's shrug was just a small shift of one shoulder. *"So, Avram still think he gonna rent?"* He frowned at the strangeness of the idea. *"Nobody want place like this now. Is good for 1972. Not now. He need look forward. Not back."*

Holding himself rigid, Avram Matteus Ider strode bravely from the aching house. In his jolliest voice, he called out, "Thanks for coming over here! Was just thinking of calling!"

The old man nodded derisively. His yellowed t-shirt, a sleeveless wifebeater, cast sharp contrast with his car's opulence but also with his obvious age. His sleepy passenger was decked just as incongruously in a faux leather jacket nearly as glossy black as the open convertible whose motor purred like a fed feline considering a playful pounce.

"Just move along. Silence! Move! Move! Look forward. Follow commands. Help me watch out for you. Go. Go

quickly! Don't slow the line!
Be wise. Be intelligent! Move!
Help me help you. Stay silent.
Just go. Look forward. Move!
Stay in line! Quietly! Quickly!
Look forward only. Move!
Believe me! Only forward.
Just go."

From both sides, out of the
night's dark cold, came
eye-stabbing lights dazing
enough to sharply enforce
harsh shouts, guttural
commands, and earnest
urgings from all directions to
look straight ahead and move
forward. And terrified,
uncramming themselves from
fetid boxcars, they moved
forward. Only forward.

GRAVITY. NO GRACE.

"Avram! Avram! When you finish? You can't move this along? Again, I say let me help you. Matuski I could send with trucks. They bring to auction, to New England, to goddam dump! Believe me. This so unnecessary. Move this along. Look forward, not back! Whachu wait for?"

"We're almost finished. Made a lot of progress today! Stan's a great helper here. I jest gotta sort this all out my own way."

"Look. You're so well fixed? You need just send kid to college? You don't know what can happen. And Sheila. She's gonna need pretty soon. The way she spend? Pretty soon!" The idea seemed wryly pleasing. And then with more mockery, *"Soon you be only man. Everything on your shoulder. Then what, huh? Huh?"*

"Everything's alright. I'm taking care of it. Ok?" Abe was smiling, but there was a glint of warning.

Shaking in anger he squeezed the bottle, farting semisweet chocolate over mounds of dark ice cream.

Spitting in his ear, she raged on. "Don't hide behind that child! Don't make like she's frightened of just me. She's frightened of THIS! Of you! Of my father. Our history. Everything!"

Refusing to look at her and refusing to answer, he scooped in another scoop,

shaking the bottle to force
forward a strong stream that
pooled up from the bottom of
the broad bowl. "You are
disgusting. That's so sick!
THAT is an addiction! You're
gonna eat all that now?
That's how you deal with
life's problems? Why don't
put on your big boy pants
and get all this settled? Don't
walk away again!"

"They won't fit over my fat
pampers," he half mumbled,
half spat. Bowl bearing, he
stumbled away. And
seething, she followed.

THERE BENEATH THE BLUE SUBURBAN SKYS

*"Look. Whaddya think you get for this place? They just knock
down and put something decent. Sell for million twenty, twenty-
five, to some damn fool. So you get six eighty? Let me help you. I
take off your hands for eight-fifty. I do what I can. She get all
anyway. You know. And Benny. I know you do right for Benny.
Benny? Benny! BENNY! Say hi to Avram! Willya, my useless
eater sweetheart?"*

"Benny!" Abe lumbered gaily to the passenger side. "Benny! Good to see ya! Pops got you out for a nice ride? Ya need a shave, Benny. Don't they shave ya at that place, Benny? Huh?"

"Hi, Abey! They shave Benny tomorrow!" Benny playfully whisked his bristly whiskers. "When you gonna visit Benny again, Abey? Benny had fun last time!"

Once they pulled away, leaving tire tracks on the lawn, Stanley turned wide-eyed to Abe. "That's him huh?"

"That's him. King of the moneyjews. Wouldn't put it past he made Roy Cohn suck him off just to givim AIDS. That's him, alright.

Stan watched the car lurch away down the road. "He doesn't get out of the car?"

Abe did not raise his eyes. "It hurts for him to walk now."

"It hurts for you to seem, doesn't it."

"Everything hurts."

*

Stacked

The pain was in his head behind his eyes, anesthetized not at all by a cloudy numbness only making it difficult to think, awkward to walk, challenging to command any limb to any bidding.

The pain was in his knees, in his neck, and in his lower back. It was in his feet and in his fingers. He considered waving a stubby pinky toward his friend and pointing to a tiny crescent below the nail. See this? he would say. It's the only part of me that doesn't hurt.

The pain was inside him and out. It was in each crate, labeled, color coded and neatly stacked, forming a tall corridor encircling the nonliving room. It was in the books piled high on each step of the way up to treacherous bedrooms and bathrooms above. It was in piles of unsorted debris on chairs, the floor, and on the couch leaving only space enough for one small crowded nest where his daughter slept every night they stayed here stuck.

It was in the basement filled with tools and casked memories: photographs, yearbooks, diaries, and mementos of schools and childhoods. It was in a tiny office still filled with logs, ad copy, books, illustrations, addresses, files and folders of deeds, transactions, and bills: some unpaid and some unsent.

It was in photos, paintings, silhouettes, and reliefs still dangling on walls. It was in statuettes, Judaica and Classical, stuffed into scalloped alcoves, now shared with whimsical debris and dead insects. It was in clippings and redolent mementos found tucked in odd crevices sometimes revealing curled, maternal, nearly indecipherable scribbles to himself or his sister.

And it was in idiosyncratic artifacts and unstylish articles of clothing, untouched and unworn since last held or fondled by an anxious mother always unmercifully driven by fear and devouring love long before and after she sickened and through the final agonies.

THE LITTLEST PARTISAN

Agonized recollections of his own marriage were another affliction. "No one helps me!" and "I don't know how!"

THE CRUSADER FOR MEMORY

The pain surrounded, compressing him, while also squeezing out mockingly from chambers hid deep inside. Mostly it was in the indecision and in each aching choice engendering new regrets for every relict retained, discarded, or put aside for additional consideration.

And then from desperation, or from a window glimpse of blue, persisting between pearlescent wisps of twisting clouds, came the prospect of escape.

"I just gotta get the hell out of here!" he rasped to a hapless friend.

*

Seventeen

On the Road Again

He found her curled in a corner reading. Bending, he uptipped her book and gave his widest big eye. Then he stood, jerked a thumb back over one shoulder, and pantomimed swerving a steering wheel. Joyously she leapt to her feet and giddy-upped the stairs, skillfully spurring an imaginary hobby horse through treacherous debris.

"Like a doggy panting for a ride," her father shrugged.

She turned a corner, kicked open the bathroom, and immediately reappeared struggling dramatically under her backpack, heavy straps clutched in both fists.

A slave's burden, its backbreaking weight swayed first in one direction and then the other. Under its unjust pressure each footstep was an agonizing trial on a steeptwisting slope of sorrows lined with loin-clothed, whip-bearing overseers and red-faced, hoarse-throated centurions brandishing bloodstained javelins, goading her ever downward to the hungry pit waiting under this stony sunbleached mount.

A surly onion-breathing rabble jeered raucously, pelting her with curses and offal. Every painful step was a delicate and perilous gamble. Would she stumble on some loose tumblesome cobblestone, or would the bones of her back or her trembling knees crumple under the strain?

> *Or, most likely, the beating heat of the sun and the throbbing ache of fresh lash wounds would soon finally overcome her wavering grip on consciousness...*

The headshaking men ushered her into the car, and together they drove smartly away.

*

Eighteen

Jew Barbecue

"Was it hard on the old man when Sarah..."

"Hey, Stan. Ya know what makes me sentimental?"

"What is it, Abe?"

"Walking by a newsstand and seeing Alfred E. Newman's still alive and kicking at freakn' limp dick trimp."

"Yeah, but him, your father-in-law?"

"I see him more, but only cuz I'm down here more with that house."

"But he came to see…" Stan nodded his head toward the child with her face in a game machine.

"How would he know we brought her here? The king of the moneyjews. He knows more Russian and Wop mobsters than the trimpster, and gets a shitload more respect from those scumbags by a long shot."

"Do you think he thinks it's his fault?"

"It wasn't his fault. For once. Sarybaby couldn't take even the hint of the idea of being exposed for being full of shit like she always wuz. She was a train wreck from the git-go and his only fault was he made her one night outta a pitcher of Slivovitz Martinis."

"But she couldn't forgive him."

"Right. But whose fault was that?" Abe smiled ravenously at the dewy young waitress and salivated over the quivering stack of ribs with sweetened iced tea. "Do the ribs come with bacon?...And anyway, forgive him for what? Surviving?"

The men ordered pulled pork sandwiches and Grendel, after energetic efforts to alert her, demanded waffles and chocolate milk.

"They don't have that here. This is a barbecue joint! You wanna hotdog?"

"I thought we were having a late breakfast brunchamunch!"

"Stanush wanted barbecue and so do I. We had breakfast this morning. Look. Chicken fingers!"

"But I told you before I wanted waffles."

"You want waffles. Stanley wants me to give him a million dollars. And I want Winona Ryder to come sit on my lap and put her tongue in my ear. You can have a hamburger here!"

"They can't make fuckin' waffles?"

"Can't you just be polite? This little girl's woikn' heeya. She gots udder people to take care of what might get snippy if she takes too long! You want Texas Toast? That's like breakfast."

"It's not waffles though."

"It's not a kick in the teat neither, but guess which one you're more likely to get in the next fifteen seconds!"

The child buried her head in her screen machine.

"Good. Give us a Texas Toast and an apple juice!"

"But I told you four times what I wanted."

"You wanted waffles and you can stuff yourself with all the freakn' waffles you want tomorrow morning. That's if I don't fill you full of cement and throw you off the ferry this afternoon."

"That's snot nice."

"**Rackem Frackem Sackum!** You wanna kill me here? You wanna take a long walk off a short pier?"

"What's a pier?"

"A peeer is someone who doesn't dribble on the toilet, at least if she's a good peeer."

"That's SNOT what he meant, Nuncle Shush! Anyway, that's what you do, Doodu!"

"A pier is like a dock. It's a wharf. It's like a bridge that doesn't make it all the way across. So if you walk too far..." Abe illustrated by walking two fingers across another and then " ...Splssssh!"

"Oh. Ha! There's no peers near here."

"So go play in traffic."

*

Nineteen

Where Ya Been All My Life?

"I'm not eating here! I wanted waffles. I told you."

"Fine. We'll get you some waffles somewhere after this. Ok? Now, can me and Uncle Stan eat the food we ordered? Look! Stan's starving! Can't you wait that long? Why not have some nice Texas Toast while you're waiting here?"

"I'll wait in the car."

"Fine. Here's the keys. ...Grezela?"

"What?"

"I'm trusting you."

"Fine."

"...Everything's wrong.

Everyone gets this. It is the way here. The ones who don't get a number...You're lucky. It hurts a little, not a lot. Just a little.

Don't make it worse. Be brave for others, can't you? Don't make it worse. Look. I have one too. Look. It's just a number. In few days, you forget. See. Needles only *scratch. Just little sore. Just little blood. See? Hold still. Brave young boy. Now the ink. It will be just little scar. We all get worse. No matter what. If we live. That's all...That's it. Behave. Get in line. Be strong.*

"Sarah's dad must be so old."

"Somewhere in his 90s. Strong. Lack bull! Has to be. Had to be. My scary Sarry just couldn't see. If he never survived, she'd never be here. She couldn't be flexible. My dad didn't judge. Everyone did what they had to. Who can judge?"

"Your wife could."

"No, Stan. Sarah couldn't. No judgment. No perspective. Total triumph or total defeat. Total righteousness or total depravity. Total eminence or total ignominy. Total innocence or total complicity. She knew better. But she didn't. Like us all. Lack us all."

"No waffling."

"No, goddamn it all to freakn' hell! Full speed ahead or

comatose in the headache room. And when everything came out, she... I even imagined it'd be like voodoo death, but my Sara was always pluck, always hadda be ahead of da curve."

"And her old man?"

"Came to the burial. Didn't talk. That's it. Not to the services. No shiva. Never a word about her. Never. He survives. He takes care of Benny. Checks in. Gives 'em hell. Moves him if they piss him off or finds a better place. That's it."

Don't dawdle! Just move. Don't look around. Keep moving! What are you going to see? What do you think? Don't think! Walk straight to where you're going. Look strong. Look like you can work! You know what happens if they think you can't work? Do you? Move smartly. Don't think. You think I won't hit you with this? Don't think. Keep moving. There's no rest. We're here now. This is it. Do

you think I won't beat you?
Do you? Keep moving! Just
keep moving.

"This can't be everything."

"It could be. All we know is what we know. Is that everything? One thing we know is we just can't take it all in. We see so little. We know so little, Stan. But is there more?"

"Abe, we have hints."

"That's all we have. Hints. What do we know about this place? This food? Have some Texas Toast? This music? Our past? Our present? Our future? Only what our brains make out from hints from our senses. Only from humane homo-nitwit genocidal frameworks for calculating concepts based on those hints."

"Things in time and space..."

"Time and space might be fake frameworks for constructing concepts. Just scaffolds required for what passes as consciousness which is mostly a systematic set of strategies for patterning a separate self."

"Huh, Abe? Say what?"

"Dimensions. They're just some basis for some quote-unquote measurements–or words for other ways of seeing... of being. That could be what's what anyway. But measurements of...? We don't know. Just deluding delusions making us think what we think we are."

"Huh? Which are?"

"I dunno, Stan. Maybe we're only our own constructs constructing what seems our idiotic selves. And each of those so-called selves, of which we all have more than one, may see everything–including *itselfs*–drastically differently."

"But we can't be *totally* different from others or ourselves?"

"No. We're bibliological orgasmisms, amongst other thangs. But whatever *that* means, it means limits. Very few of us think we're aardvarks or lawn chairs. But then again... Sometimes I think I'm a nematode. Hit the road, Jack."

"Right, Abe. Sometimes I think trimp is a Vogon."

"The thing is... if spacetime's a delusion, some mathematical construct, then there's no separate nematodes, aardvarks, or killer whales. We're just one big *thang*. One big thing with more dimensions than we generally sense. Except if we think of this manifold as a *thing*, we're just word-trapping ourselves. Delusions we can't *thang* ourselves out of."

"And, Abe! We aren't even selves."

"Goddamn it. Why didn't I say that?"

"Because you're not an eye?"

"Eye cunt hear you cuz I'm not an ear."

"You cunt. I'm not a queer."

"I killed a cat and Schrödinger can't know it."

"McTavish is dead and his brother don't know it."

His brudder is dead and Mick Stanush don't show it."

"OHHHH!"

"But Stan, we have our senses! Maybe more than just the proverbial five. Maths and logic might be senses too. Like in mathematics you can work with tons of dimensions."

"So, you're saying senses might be coming out of us, out of our minds instead of just into our brains from what seems outside? Math and logic might be like that?"

"Maybe a moral sense too. Out from minds between our selves. Outside minion minds and beyond selfish selves, but also woven through the endless fabric of what we call life: Nature: Physics. Maybe."

"So Abe, are you saying language can't assign names to *those* senses because they're less keen than the ones scarred into us through the tattoos of evolution?"

"Maybe language is more than a scaffold for building concepts? Maybe it's one of the scaffolds for building new senses."

"To help pick out impressions from dimensions we can't name."

"Universes, Stan. Universes! ...If senses just gather hints, and language is part of that hinting system, then maybe music and poetry are too. Especially music. And every new sense-system doesn't just find new dimensions, they might be building new universes! Infinitely!...Here. Just take the card. I don't need to see the bill."

"Oh, I think I see," intervened Stan to distract the hulking hellhound from its quavering prey. "And where are all the turtles?"

"They're all slavering after the prawns."

But basset-hound eyes followed the blushing server as she rushed to weave herself away between crowded tables. They turned pleadingly to Stan whom Abe queried, "...Were *we* ever that young? Were *we* never that beautiful?"

*

Twenty

The Edge of the Known Universe

"..alls I knew bout religion growing up was People of the Boo. He would have none of it, my poor widda tattoo dad. But spook at us now. My sis Shelia, a dizzy frum diddy, and me generatin' me own."

 Joe Panzica

"Yeah... Your dad's books. ...His imagination. Pretty quirky."

"Comfort or creation."

"Hmm?"

"His kid innocence got stripped by human monstrosity. But he didn't want all children should be so deprived. An escape for his own jitters."

"So Sarah's dad clutched after wealth and influence? Your pops cultivated creativity and whimsy?"

"Listen, Stoon. My dad sucked up moneylove as much as anybody. He'd never of retired without a lot socked. Always nabbing reassurance. More, probably, than most grubbers who never survived such a clutch of human depravity. Organized legitimated murderous depravity. But maybe tried not to victimize himself. Maybe. Most of the time. Maybe he needed to beat them that way. Scarab's dad, in his never imminent dotage, consorts still with the worst fiends and deatheaters in the US of freaking A, Israel, Europe, Latin America and, for all I know, Africunt, Malasia, Asstraila, and Antique Icicle too. What's that all about? Embracing the dark side? Facesucking the fear?"

"You think *your* dad found peace? Denied victimizers victory over his soul?"

"His what? Who does that, Stan? Who finds peace?"

"I guess."

"But he protected his kids best he could. Ways not too crushing. See it clearer now. What's the saying? Consider no man happy who still lives? My father. Always draped under morose. But maybe his happy moments were more blissful than whatever passes for crap fulfillment in today's mainstream sewer pipes."

"There's gotta be some bit of truth there."

"Hmmm. Some bitter truth. But, waddabout his kids? Sheila and me? We're clearly ducking idiots. A wonder we can feed ourselves. And what about his grand spawn? Two moneyhumpen gran-chicos who think they're bros in hip-hop kippots and a tone-deaf granddaughter spectrum stuck with the likes of me and a gonegirl muddster who..."

"You know what, Abe? I think she's gotta good chance. Internal resources! Just keep hanging in the best you can."

"I never know what that means. Shelter her? Let her

discover life's horrors on her own? Expose her in a vaccinatory way?"

"She's getting toward that age, Abe."

"Getting? Have you been paying attention? She's there, Stan. Sure, she's tiny and acts it. Very freakn' immature. But she's way past the bloody event horizon."

"So you're going through with it this time?"

"I don't know. When's sheltering jest stunting? Her Abba always wanted to. Was always trying. Wouldn't let him. For her? For me? But now? Look what she's carrying round already! Of course, I don't wanna have to see her take it in. But if she shrugged it off? No reaction? What would that mean? All for the best? Healthy denial? Waiting for some time bomb? Maturity? Or she's just another dud? She's not. No matter what she isn't, she's not no dud."

"She sure goes off."

"A lot."

"So tomorrow?"

"Yeah! The impairing unveiling. With Grets, it's imp trailing. Always gunning her motor. Hope I don't choke her... Buts it's jest a nether story. Another freakn' story. Only not like John and Yokahoma Mama's. Six million plus Dakotas is alls it is. A couple bakers' dozen Hiroshimas with the fallouts still fallin like stars scarring Alabama, falling down on us, dusting us, caking us, mudding us up for generations to cum upon."

"She's strong Abe. More resilient than you think. I know I see it."

"You think so, Stan? You really think so? Count no person...while they breathe."

Stan waited several moments before he knew it was all on him to nudge his friend up and out the door to go find his little girl.

*

Part III

The Cruelest Month

Twenty-One

Three Generations of Imbeciles

In some ways, it all started here.

Was it Watson or Crick? Crick or Watson? Which?

...Way before them.

Vannevar? W's great grand illegitimate step-uncle? What happened? Natural degeneration of lineage, no doubt.

Way before him too. I think.

An empty campus. Nobody walking around. Are the buildings empty too? Who put the cars here?

Like in The Prisoner or The Avengers. Eerie Britishy empty expanse. Not too sinister though. Not without the right music or camera angles.

Still, wouldn't want to get out of the car.

> *Excuse me, sir. Can I help you? Have you ID? What's your business here? Come with me, please. Now, now. Take it easy, Sir. Just making sure everything is what it should be. Don't now make a fuss now. It's all for the greater good, you know.*

Billy Joe Cold Spring Harmer.

Manicured fertilized grassy green greensward. Pleasant-looking buildings.

There's someone. Tweedy. Waspy. No Jews

allowed. Only the masterful race. We will teach your blue-eyed speech. To the unbelievers.

I wonder if cell phones work here? It was easy to drive in. But waddabout driving out? They need fresh meat. Fresh blood. Fresh genes.

"Dr. Moreau? Calling Dr. Moreau. Did he arrive at Building C yet? He's left a liver on the floor in G again." *People with ears on their butts living underground.* One of us. One of us. GabbaGabba. Pleased to meetchew. Gabba Gabba. Gabba. Hey. Gobble.

Buck v. Bell. Bell v. Buck? If Vannevar led to a W, could Carrie B. have led to an O. W? Holmes? Feeble-minded. There's one in every home. Everyone's family tree has a few blistered buds. I should know.

Carrie Buck or Carrie Bell? I think she was white, but they did mostly blacks. I suppose they did white girls who might go for black bucks too. Can't blame 'em, can you? It really was all about race. It didn't start here. And race was about colonies and slavery.

It didn't start here.

Slavery which is profit and rape and torture had to be justified. It built us up. Cotton. Cheap for a globular market. The structures we stand on. Warps us still. Blood poured in Civil War didn't atone. Our spirit wasn't changed, wasn't cleansed. And the evil bled down generations strange and far. The blue-eyed, white-faced, master race. We teach your twisted speech. Profit. Has to be paid for. Debits must balance credits.

It didn't start here. It spread from here. NAZIs ate it up. Maximum Millions Schnell splained all it to Sphincter Tracy. And poor Montgomery Cleft, the poor stuttering little jew bastard. Never hurt no body! And poor Judy Garland? Did they do her? And Toto too?

My father was a good-looking kid. Strong. That helped. But good-looking helped more. Shouldn't matter but does. I was good-looking too. Once. Helped. She's good-looking. In a way. Hope it helps. Shouldn't matter but. Always brush your teeth. Always comb your hair. Change your bloody underwar cuz you jest can never know.

Got her nose in her machine. Better

scenery. Doesn't get carsick. Doesn't look out window. If she listens to her pappy, good people, she won't know up from down. When she gets to the bottom, she'll go back to the top of the tribe. But when she gets to the bottom good people, will she ever see me again?

But what does it matter? What does matter matter?

She matters.

Our self-consciousnesses are quivering illusory protrusions from some more fundamental source being sourced unfundamentally. Right? Check? Roger that, Nigel? Please confirm. Please confirm. Please.

Why you gotta teller?

Separations and divisions are not real. So neither is pain nor fear. Or at least our conceptions of them are fatally blinkered. Our human-type consciousness is not so special as we think. Speck of something grander. Expander.

It's all that matters to me now. She's gotta know. And she'll discover anyway. What's my job?

Daddyman.

A love supreme. Our all. Sound waves,

thought waves, light waves, night waves, all vibrations, all words, all men, all memory, fears, and time. All from one. Love-supreme heaving through us completely, weaving us so sweetly. We don't feel it. So roughly it unfurls us. So powerfully it hurls us.

A love supreme. One thought emits a zillion butterfly vibrations. All go back to love supreme. Everything does. Love supreme. It don't come easy. No road does. Why don't we do it? But they all, long and winding, go back to love supreme. Everything does. A love supreme.

It's all that matters to me now, but someday I'll be forced to let it go. I just had to...

What will it do to her?

Everybody blends together in the end though I know I'll never lose affection. And when I am done and buried, good people, with my face turned to the sun, would you stand and moan for my pretty little girl, and think what I have done? My father was of the sky, good people. My mother was of the world. And I am of the loony verse and I don't know which is worse.

Nobody told you how to unfurl your love. We were all diverted. All perverted. Almost all our love is sleeping. Only sleeping. Don't wake me. Don't break me. Can't you see?

So many years I was searching good people. So many tears I cried to the ground. Now I can see you and be you, my baby, but I'll only let you down.

It's all that matters to me now, but someday I'll just have to let her go.

If you grow to be a singer, my baby, wearing bling and things, don't worry about what I say. Live and shove and maybe some fine day, you'll find a love half right. Laugh right's only half of what's wrong. I'll always love a short-haired girl who just might tear hers wrong. Glad. So glad. So glad? I am. Am I?

Everything blends, and all you need is love. What we call entropy: ultimate balance. What we call gravity: primitive cumulation. And we tend to think they're separate. But nothing is. And money can't buy me love. There are only unities we can't sense cuz they make no sense to our *slivered minds. We're only the sleeping. It tears us apart. And hurts.*

Entropy blends by spreading out. Gravity by pulling tight. Every thang's sub-energy twisting into or tearing apart.

But it's all blending and expansions. Expanding and concentrations. Out of our glimpses.

In to and out from new dimensions.

New loonyverses.

What we observe's only a flick of a filament in an ever-expanding milkyiverse, a thin twist of a swirl in a vaster whirl. A tiny twit of a girl. She expands into everything. Why?

She's all that matters to me now, but in a while she'll make me let her go.

How will I say it?

They murdered your great grandcestors with plans, machinery, and science. Nearly got your grandcrawdaddies: your Zeyde, your Obby. And might yet come for you. Maybe from you. Then they were only sleeping. ***It*** *was* only...half of what I say is...

It's waking! It's waking, *and what if somehow she knows?*

Now it rumbles everything.

> *Turtles all the way down. Turtles all the way up. Turtles all the way out. Turtles all the way in.*

Did I say turtles all the way out?

> *Turtles expanding. Turtles contracting. Turtles shimmering in and out, between, and through each which are never really other.*

> *All turtles containing every. All turtles within each. And there is no other.*

> *We all shine on.*

The talk. Black parents gotta have theirs. About cops. About whites. About us. About me.

For us though... For warmed is forlorn. For armed is tattooed. For us.

Call it love, but not watered-down. Diluted's all we can take. But only spreads inside our minds where space and time reside. Concentrated, it burns more than a bush. More than Vannevar. What creates, destroys. Love Supreme, but no twang is

ever lost. Not our watered-down mindlessness with blind word-bound protrusions.

Space spreads us all apart. Time do two. Separateness is our awareness: a step, not in time. Creation is everything creating. A Love Supreme. We curl always into our selves and blow them apart. We all shine on.

I'm fixing a whole what keeps my mind from wondering, and it really doesn't matter if I'm wrong. I fight. And I really have to shout and leap about. This love of mind keeps groaning all the time.

Blink for yourself. It's all you can do. And someday you won't be blotted out. Cuz we'll all shine on. Like Venus and Mars and Happiness is a Warm Gun. We all shine on.

Come on everyone. Everyone come on.

* * *

There was a crush of a great mind silence over-imposing the customary static and crosschat. It had pressed grand Avram, the father of frustrations, to pull over and stall.

"Uh, Abey?" Stan's voice needled in from the passenger seat. "I don't think we can park here."

Abe slowly, almost reluctantly, released his grip on the steering wheel. He stared at his friend trying to make out what had just been said. "You're right," he croaked. "I dunno why I wanted to see dis place." The empty vastness made his voice ring hoarse and harsh and uncertain. "But how much you wanna bet my sister will be late to the boneyard?"

Abe Ider checked the girl in his rearview and drove them out of Cold Spring Harbor. To no one in particular he remarked, "And to think this place was always here so close to where I grewed up."

*

Twenty-Two

The Knapsack

Before they got two steps, Gretchen turned around. She tugged at the rear passenger door and looked up expectantly.

"You don't really need that now," came a parental reproach, more a whine than a warning.

She tugged more insistently. He clicked it open. She struggled into the knapsack, running to catch up with her father and her father's friend.

They stood in a V with the girl the point. She could reach out and touch the stone. *"They put the wrench on it."* Her voice was careful. *"It lines up with the rifle on Mamie's side."*

"Mamie," murmured Abe Ider, repeating his daughter's invented name for his mother whom she'd never met.

"I wanna rifle carved into my gravestone too. A big one."

"You should never have one."

"But you never know, Papoop. You tell stories about Mamie being a partisan in the woods, but you never say much about Obbie. You wouldn't let him talk. You'd yell at him. You wouldn't even let him tell Stanoosh."

"He'd want me to talk when you're ready."

"I'm ready now."

"He'd want me to talk when I'm ready."

"I heard that man say Obbie dropped grenades on the Arabs. Is it that?"

"No. That's only one story to tell."

"Ok. Tell me."

"Your auntie's coming soon with the veil. So this isn't a good time. Later when we go to the place I might talk."

"Is it sad stories? Was Obbie bad?"

"Do you think your grandfather was bad?"

"No. Then it's sad. He always seemed a little sad."

"Yup."

"I know. I know what it was. I just don't know the stories."

She took off her knapsack and pushed it up fast against the stone, standing it perpendicular to the grass.

"Remember it looked like they couldn't fit him into the hole? That was funny. I thought we'd have to dig."

"I thought we'd have to dig."

"I started crying because I didn't want him to go down there."

"Everybody was sad, but it was his time."

She touched the stone. She touched the rifle and read the inscription below:

THE LITTLEST PARTISAN

"They made a movie about that. But Mamie wasn't in it."

"No. But her Anty, your great aunt, was though they changed the name. She lives still in Israel and you might meet her someday."

"Is she nice?"

"Very nice. And she'd be very very pleased to see you and hug you and kiss you and cook for you."

"But she's old."

"Very old."

"And she might die first."

"If her time comes."

She touched the wrench. Then her knapsack. Then she touched the wrench again and sprinted off.

The two men watched her run.

"At least she left the knapsack," observed her father sadly.

They watched her zigzag between graves in ever-widening circles around their forsaken nucleus, often ducking behind a stone, peeping up to make sure they were still watching, blinking in and out of existence.

*

Twenty-Three

A Love Supreme

Sheila arrived late, towing a friend, expressing ostentatious annoyance her brother had, too early, already approached the stone.

When pleading shouts did not avail, a frozen silent pose enforced by glancing daggers eventually pulled the orbiting child into their thawing tableaux.

The stone was draped. Prayers were chanted by Sheila (earnestly) and her friend (gamely). Sad sighing Abe made intermittent, somewhat histrionic, attempts to disguise false boredom and genuine irritation. Stan, mostly successfully, strove to present as solemn and respectful. It worked best if he avoided the insistent attempts at eye contact from the fat man. Gretel, intrigued, tried to apprehend them as a group, as individuals, and as dyads and triads.

Then, drawn to the marker, she experienced it as something again new. The wrench and the rifle were merely prominent symbols in a multitude of glyphs.

New words popped into her eyes. On the rifle side was "Bielski Brigade" and "Belarus". On the wrench side was "Auschwitz" and "Haganah." She reached for her father's well-padded hand.

Arrangements were made for a later meeting at Sheila's new favorite deli and a subsequent caravan to the Memory Center. They then split in oblique angles towards their respective vehicles, each taking its own separate trajectory and momentum.

* * *

Enduring intense Abe Ider speeds and sharp Abe Ider veers, backseat Greta remarked on the impressive expanse of another cemetery strobing past their velocity. Its diagonal columns of identical stones stretched out toward a distant tree line and far beyond.

"It's a Vet's Cemetery," Stan explained. "The largest in the country. World War I, World War II, Korea, Vietnam, Kuwait, Iraq, Afghanistan, and others and others, and on and on." The girl, knapsack hugged in her lap, pushed her nose to shatterproof glass, and stared.

Eventually, in Abe's muscle car they penetrated a third graveyard, one of normal dimensions and demeanor. Here trees thrust themselves up randomly, the browned grassy ground was unleveled, and markers were allowed idiosyncrasies.

"Here it is!" cried Abey after an apparently frantic, but actually quite systematic search. He lumbered as rapidly as possible back to the car where he was irascibly perturbed to find someone had removed a pair from the twelve-battery boombox.

"Look how many it still has!" someone provocatively quipped.

With a James Cagney sneer, her father made a Jimmy Cagney fist. And then, Cagney James-like, he twisted an imaginary grapefruit into his daughter's expectant upturned face. He put the CD into the car, turned up the volume, and opened wide the doors.

The other two watched as, in front of this grave, Abe stood in a silent and respectful stance.

"His house is not far," Abe recited. "And neither is the hospital where he died in '67."

Abe made them listen long enough to be unmistakably late for their delicatessen date.

* * *

A high wind blew, drawing warmth upward from the graves and the grass. It bent the treetops. The girl danced to her own music. Her father swayed to his.

Lurid sunlight pushed ferociously through cloudslits straining to clench themselves closed. A pressure shift, a sudden rain smell, and a looming sky drama combined to vitalize the dancers; the girl pirouetting and the father bobbing, loose necked and bouncy knees. Slim Stanley stretched back against a treetrunk scratching dryskin shoulders through his shirt, writhing with crucified pleasure and anxiety. The music pulsed.

And then heavy drops, seasonably cold, plopped singly, darkly, randomly, percussively, falling oblivious to the waltzing gusts or to the elation, elegance, and exaltation of the sounds.

"Acknowledgment", "Resolution", "Pursuance", and "Psalm."
"Worship", "Universality", "Creation", and "Gratitude."
A Love Supreme

Unlucky Lindy's

From the moment they walked in, she knew it'd be no good. Now it was nothing but bad.

Silence used to comfort. So many ways to be enfolded, with ground sounds almost as soothing. Once, even plugged in, it had been nothing to lean into or away from musical confusion, distant shouts and voices, traffic noise, or the buzzdrone of adult chatter.

None of it made much sense. Even big-eye talk.

Just big-eye them back, nod, and maybe smile sometimes. It mostly worked. Later you could say you didn't understand or didn't remember. Now they expected you to listen even when they weren't making with the eyes.

More and more, if she needed soothe, she had to switch off. Adult talk was more disturbing and rougher to ignore. Except lately she could feel pressed in silence as well.

Anty's cool face was smug, her voice smooth. Her father's sweaty one was reddening. There was that clip to his words. She tried to focus on her gamey thingy, but it no longer absorbed.

"You obviously don't know anything about the importance of social adaptation."

"Ya think I want her adapting? She'll figure out people

soon enough and know she never missed nuttin. She's doing fine."

"But she's totally missing out in all sorts of ways. You have an obligation as a parent."

"Parent? Don't parent me, Shmeilia. Look how your pointy-eared ones turned out for gadzamighty frugging crissakes!"

"Please. Aaron is in mergers and acquisitions and Arye's interning on the stock exchange."

"Right. Two dim minions of casino capitalism! And you're happy with that?"

Gretchen disconnected. The gamey thing was nothing. She considered throwing it across the room or at someone's head. But what if she hurt someone? She didn't want another hospital.

She could throw it on the floor. Smash it to sharp shards. Dadzilla would be mad, but soon enough he'd getter a cooler tablet which he shoulda anyway, the cheapo creepo.

A certain waiter kept catching her eye. Slim and small, he skated from table to table, smoothly picking up and putting down, counting back change, and reciting specials as if gliding through a cloudfooted dream. She checked again. No skates. Sleepwalking? No, sleep dancing, his face as calm as a ballerina's. She'd never seen anyone like that.

Beyond the window lay what Stan had pointed out as they bickered in the parking lot. A smelly cheese man had flown a plane from there across an ocean for the very first time. Then someone kidnapped his baby and killed it. Now it was a bunch of shopping malls.

Shmelia and her pointy-boobed friend didn't care, but Stanush and Dadush had worried whether Cheese Pilot was a Nazi or not.

Not. They decided, but.

She didn't want to be taken away from her father or from Carol Ann and Stan. They might put her in a home where a boy could put a baby in her. She wondered about being a boy. They could put babies in a dozen girls a night for weeks and not even know. No matter what they all said, she didn't think she could get a baby yet. But—what if?

If it came out a ringtail, it was Rocky Racoon's.

If it was hairy all over, it was Spurious George's.

Still, boys weren't much better than girls. If at all.

Some men were good. But even good ones could be scary. Not that she'd let them know though.

*

Twenty-Five

Sea of Monsters

Heading toward the bathrooms, she stopped herself in a chamber glassed on three sides.

It was set off from the dining areas by vitreous dessert cases. None of the chocolate ones were nearly dark enough to entice but sealed behind crystal were lots of creamy things: banana, lemon, cherry, vanilla: all puffy, swirls and parfait. They sat towered, stacked, and shelved, some in tall transparent tubes turning slowly in a rotation intended to be tempting.

Two other plates overlooked parking. Through one she could make out the long-gone airfield now flattened under malled sprawl. But it was raining. While she watched, the drops grew bigger, fell faster, and finally commingled into swift slanting sheets dashing against the glass.

At first, it was like gawking into an aquarium. Then her perch became The Great Glass Elevator submerging into a storm-topped sea. But she could imagine no fish. Instead were puppies and kittens, raccoons and rabbits, dolls, tricycles, and Teddy Bears. Some floating serenely. Some swimming frantically. Some simply paddling in a slightly frolicsome way. But all were sunk below the water's rim, engulfed in a deluge too grand for them to understand.

She pushed her palms against the glass which seemed to melt into the rippling curtains of rain pelting heavily against them.

Then she was outside, submersively drenched.

And she ran.

She shot down a sidewalk into an intersection, making the center median before lights changed and swift dashing traffic marooned her. Then lights changed again. Three lanes idled anxiously between her and the diner side, but she couldn't go back. The beyond was splashy as traffic made swerving left turns, whipping water into her hair and eyes. And when that finally quieted, she was cold and too fearful to risk stepping onto the puddling tar. So, there she stood.

She stood long enough for panic to subside and to notice the rhythm of the signaled streams hurtling by. Eventually, she could sprint one way or the other, but that meant choosing a side to dart to. And the water was so cold.

* * *

Avram Ider, sitting, munching, blustering, and fencing dry inside, eventually got edgy.

He dragged himself to the atrium and plodded back to prod his sister to roust the little lady's room. She came back tensed and wild-eyed. Following a spurt of jittery milling, they all pressed together out into the wet where they screeched and bellowed the missing child's name.

After more scrambled confusion, Abe saw her first.

Like a dreadnaught Moses, ignoring squealing brakes and venomous horns, he plowed through the lanes of streaming projectiles and, panting, gathered his limp girlchild into shaking arms.

"What are you trying to do to me?" was all he thought to say.

*

Twenty-Six

Snot Girl

Dripping, they dragged themselves to their cars.

Usurping the lead, Sheila swooped first out of the lot, her friend frantically fitting the belt. But within three Long Island traffic lights she fell fast behind hard-driven Abe who kept her blocked until, finally, she seemed to relent.

"Who's the best singer you know?"

"You aren't, Nunco Stashu."

Damp Abe groaned and farted in an attempt at pre-emptive harmony.

"Just let 'em have it, Stanoodu."

"That's Stanudo Croonruso to you, Simp. Anywho:
   My rhino it seems had fractured her schemes
   by spreading the legs of his snot girl
   Her name was Red Lil, and she called herself Bill
   but everyone knew her as Nigel."

"You sound like a coyote, and no girl is named Bill."

Abe turned around. "The duck they're not. What about Lady Day?"

"What about Gilda the Good? What about Ringo?"

"Ringo's not a girl."

He sang 'Boys'!"

"So."

"Ok. Billy Shears snot a girl or a redeemable bill. But this song's about a snot girl."

"Ok. I a snot boy."

"Sometimes you're snot cute," contributed Fat Dad.

"Sometimes I snot nice. Anyway 'Nigel' doesn't rhyme."

"My innocent child. Poems don't have to rhyme since 1932. Ask Extra Pounds! But *jell* rhymes anyway sideways with hard g *snot Gell*."

"What rhymes with Streamly Gredible?"

"How 'bout 'Unseemly Upsettable'?"

"How 'bout 'Screaming Petrel'?"

"How 'bout 'Obscenely Edible'?"

"How 'bout 'Pantingly Pettable'?"

"Woof! Roof! Woof woof Woof!"

"Ahhrroooof! Oooof woof woof whoooeee! Hiyihiyee Awhoooo!"

"Yip yip yip yip, yipowowowooo!"

"Awhooo! Woof Woof Woof Ahrooo!"

And Avram Ider, gripping his wheel, sitting stiffly, driving straight ahead, thrusted forward by family stabs behind and before, growled and growled and growled long after the coyotes had settled themselves down.

*

Twenty-Seven

Butterflies Are Not Free

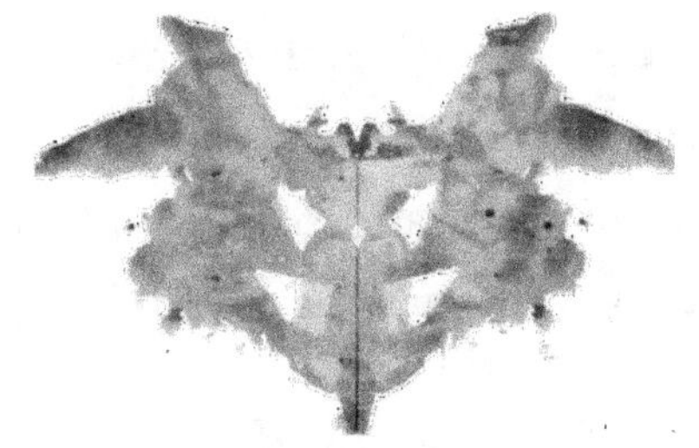

They were late.

In fact, the place was closed.

Two official women were locking up. Luckily, or unfortunately according to perspective, one of the lockers was the director.

Imperious Sheila drew on her every reserve of intensity, pleading, and entitlement to explain her father, this particular child's grandfather, had been a survivor, a former docent: a benefactor with a butterfly to prove it. The others shuffled uncomfortably, glared menacingly, or cultivated innocent oblivion.

They were admitted. In Gretchen's memory, the soft grey labyrinths inside would always be hard and soot black. Stanley, on his first visit, found himself choking before initiatory photographs of children frozen.

The inner maze was a mosaic of blacks and grays. Through their constituent pixels, the children, blown up, were still sharply imaged. Dotmottled boys and girls were still irredeemably immersed in the immediacy of childlife with toys, booksacks, uniforms, frowns, and smiles; their curiosities, anticipations, anxieties, and vacancies pinned. History, which seemed to these survivor-scarred memorialists to be an overwhelming shockwave inexorably hurtling them futureward with no sweet prospect of shelter, was to those still children absurdly inconceivable.

Gretel, shut off in silence, desultorily pretended to study, briefly, any of a random sample of placards apparently arresting one or another adult. When grownups formed a hushed coven before one particular photo, she saw gestures for her to join. But, their phalanx creating for her no sufficient opening, she turned–and briskly, quickly, intently, strode away.

Later, beneath a high grey sky, as they stood before the Obbyfly, the Arch Patriarch Avram Solemn Man kneeled before her and reverently tapped the back and sides of her head, fixing her eyes with uncommon intensity.

Ritually, she pressed her magnetic headside switch.

> "...he was only thirteen, you know. Big for his age like you're small. They got a warning and sheltered on a farm nearby with a family who'd bought their lumber for years and years. It was their only chance, and they shivered there a few days in a shed built for animals."

He stopped for any reaction or question.

> "But the mother turned them in. Obby's brother and father ran into the woods when the soldiers came. They were shot.

They kept Obby in the shed another cold night with his mom. Then they took them. He never saw his mother again."

His words, at first measured, became quick and bitter. Gretchen shook her head and closed her eyes. She covered her ears, a gesticulation never before deployed.

"I know. "

"Sorry. I'm sorry," Abe numbly repeated, wondering at his immense capacity for error.

"I know. And the earth is methane burning too. I know." **The little girl froze. Only her eyes were wild.**

Hard-angled Sheila, making herself soft, pulled "wittle gretten" into an approximation of solace that only eventually became uncomfortable.

They sat on hard courtyard benches. The director ceased hovering and brought out bottles of water and cans of ginger ale. None of the chilled crowd refused; insisting she join the drinking. After quiet talk of plans for the Center and benign stories of acquaintances made common by its functioning, the director excused herself for some very important calls and paperwork.

There was a long moment.

Alone, Gretchen walked back to the Obbyfly.

Moishe Ider
1930 - 2015
Auschwitz II–Birkenau
1944-1945

There was nothing about sawmills, studies, languages, parents, grandparents, aunts, uncles, or brothers. Nothing about Israel, Haganah, airplanes, or grenades. Nothing about plumbing supply. Nothing about hobbies, stories, or strange structures of PVC. Nothing about being a docent. Nothing about a son or a daughter. Nothing about grandsons. And nothing about a granddaughter.

Obby's was one of many butterflies, all with the same manner of names and dates. She faced her father who with moist eyes slowly approached. She pushed herself into his immense mass.

After a while, she looked up into his penitent face.

After another while, he spoke, hesitantly. "I was wondering if maybe this was a good time for something else."

She stared back, feeling much younger, like the smaller child she had forgotten once was her.

"You don't have to, but I was wondering if this was a good time to, you know, let her rest. You can scatter her here. We can help. We can be quiet. We can pray. We can sing. We can even dance and laugh. Nobody but we all has to know. We can come back whenever you want."

He waited.

Her eye contact was solid. She gave no sign she heard, no sign she was listening, no sign she was considering, and no sign if she were about to bolt. She didn't move. Her eye contact was solid.

"She'd like to be here with Obby's spirit which is in this place, not the cemetery. It would make her happy. Whatever you think, she wouldn't want you carrying her forever."

After another pause, he dropped his gaze and waited some more.

"I'm gonna carry her some more."

Now her eyes dropped. She shuffled her feet. She

pulled tighter the straps of her knapsack and slow walked, then rapid trotted, back into the labyrinths.

*

Twenty-Eight

Another Cut

Farflung Farther Able, shaking his head in an un-forced display of confused regret, addressed his muted audience. "Sometimes I just don't know what's wrong with me."

Slowly he circled them before glumly plodding into the grey tomb that had swallowed whole his only daughter.

He found her puzzling the photo they had beckoned her to see and hovered paternally above her right shoulder.

"*Who are they?*"

"See that girl in the middle?"

She nodded.

"See those scissors in her hand?"

She peered closely. "*Uh-huh.*"

"We have those. You've held them in your hand."

She looked up at him.

"That's my mother. That's your grandmother."

She turned again to study the girl in a white dress standing casually among others so dressed in various formal states of posed busyness; the only girl addressing the camera. It was like a hair salon, only it wasn't.

"She's in a relocation camp. It's about a year after the war. They're teaching her a trade."

"*Did Obby put this here?*"

"Not that I know of. He said he found it here in this spot just like you did. He couldn't believe it. I can't either. Of all the pictures in all the places this could have turned up."

"*So he's here, and she's here too.*"

"**Yup.**"

"*That's why you want I should put Mommy here too?*"

"**You don't have to.**"

"*Maybe.*"

She put out a faint finger to press against the ghost of curly hair floating above the ghost of a clumsy smile.

"*Someday.*"

She took his hand and together they walked out into a lighter shade of grey.

*

Twenty-Nine

Aftermath

That was supposed to be it.

But we didn't all go home. We took a walk instead, but not a hike because Sheila and her girlfriend didn't have good shoes. I saw Daddoo and Schmelia talking nice and Stanasauce and Schmeliafriend too. Then they were talking about my Mudd and being dead and when we were gonna finally finish sorting out the Obbyhouse. Then Fatty Daddy caught me listening and they stopped.

We even went together to another deli that wasn't kosher this time. Anty said it was fine cuz she wasn't hungry anyway cuz we had lunch so late and her friend ordered a salad. Daddy had bacon on his cheeseburger and took it out like was a cigar and he was Groucho. Shelia's friend told Stanley she didn't mind getting on her knees once in a while for a good cause and he said his barber was very quick and she always gave him quickies. I wonder what Carol Ann's gonna say when I tell her?

But after a while, Shiela only talked to her friend and Doopu only talked to Stoopu. The ladies talked about something while the mens talked about who was hotter and cuter. Stanoopy said Debra Winger was both and Dadzukes said it was Winona Ryder. Then the womens talked about something else but the mens talked again about the Beatles. John and Paul were both protons. George was a neutron, but that meant he was just as powerful even if he was more quieter. And Ringo was the gluon that kept them all together.

I know that means they're helium. I had two milkshakes. Then finally we did all go home.

Later Danoodu said Smelia's friend was a cupid stunt and I know that means "See you next Tuesday" and that snot nice. So I said he should talk like how intelligent he really was, and as soon as I said that I knew it wasn't me. That was something Mudder used to say and it was her voice too, not mine, even in the sound of it. The way Daddu looked at me, I knew he knew it too.

*

Part IV

Simmering Summer Kills

Thirty

Here's Mud in Your Thigh

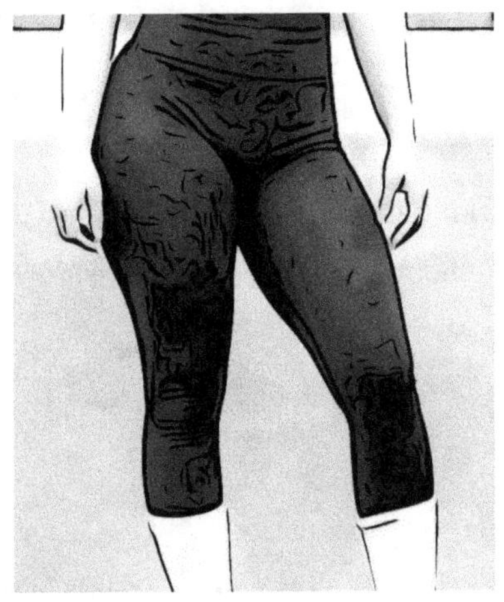

Zlottie says her mummy in Poland was a doctor. She spent every weekend cooking stuff for them to eat all week like stuffed cabbage which is yummy, pierogies which take too long to make, zernina which is disgusting, kuglies *which she is going to show me how, and* chepeleenay *which also sounds super good.*

Obby told me his Mudd was a good cook too. She hardly knew how to read but knew lots of stories. When they were in the sheep pen, I bet she kept him warm even though she was shivering herself.

Doody says his Mutt watched TV and went to doctors too much. But she was always good to him even though she always said annoying things. When she had cancer, he took care of her every night and day until she died.

Nuncoo Stupo says his Musser was very nervous, and that after she died his father told him he was her favorite.

Carol Ann says her Mammal was in and out of the nuthouse and always took more pills than her doctors wanted. I think that's why she likes to take care of me.

My mudder didn't like me which is streamly gredible. Doodoo says she loved me though. But I don't know. She's not here. Not really.

*

Thirty-One

Sea of Holes

"Abe, think what you're doing! You outta your freak-ing mind?"

"I dunno."

"When are you gonna get another invitation to record again? And in London? At Abbey Freaking Road?"

"I know. With the Kugelspud Quartet. My only one chance to fondle the Strawberry Fields harmonium."

"Well. Come on!"

"Yeah, but waddabout the weight I gotta carry if I don't go do this other thing now? Chaos in my own backyard! A march of the cocksuckn' meanies!"

"It's not up to you."

"Look!" Abe pushed a screen under his friend's face. "See for yourself! Who is it up to? What's it all about? It's not getting better on its own. Everybody's gotta do something! Whaddam I gonna say to the kid when she asks me later what I did?"

"What you think you're gonna accomplish there? You gonna punch a fascist in the face? It's just a bunch of nitwits. You got something positive to offer. That counts more!"

"I dunno... I dunno. Tina Fey ate all the sheet cake. Maybe I'll throw confetti at them. Maybe there's an anti fatshit comedy group that needs a bluborous straight man. Maybe I could dress up as Goering? Was he the fattest? And I could ride a tricycle with a clown nose? A bubbly red balloon strung to my dick? I dunno. I am old and no good."

"Don't say that, Abe. You're a year younger than I am."

"Sary was a shitty mother, but I was a shitty husband. And I'm a pathetic pieceofcrap excuse for a father."

"Come on. This doesn't help."

"And this. This! This is my fault too. All of us. We've been slurping in capitalist urinals. We've been sleeping. We've been sleepwalking, and these broken, godforsaken, empty, ignorant, smutaddled schmucktards are not the only zombies. They are not the only ghouls. I'll find a Sid Caesar doorman and buy his outfit off him. Money, I got. That's it for now. That's all I gotz. I never earned it. And I never do any good with it."

"Ok. Ok. OK. Cycles! Turn Turn Turn. A seasonal time for every elastic, as you would say, sleazy ass thing. This is how the universe swirls. It hurts some time. You know that. Use your brain. Use your imagination! This is the time to create! Don't get sucked into that sewer!"

"I dunno. This hurts bad, ya know. Bad."

"OK, Abe. Jest lemme go with you on the Common then for fug's sake. This could be a short hot summer."

"You can't do that. It sucks enough I gotta leave that girl with Carrie. You gotta help her."

"No. Carrie's a force unto herself. And then the more people where you're going the better. They can't do this."

"No. Not again."

*

Thirty-Two

Free Speech

Gracie leaned harder against her, pushing in between her legs. Marbles, lounging lazily in a corner bed, thumped drowsily.

"Bread takes a long time to make at home. Pierogi's even harder."

"Could you push that bowl away from the edge, please?

"Cookies are easier to make. And they taste better at home."

"Every time you touch that dog, you better wash your hands. Homemade bread tastes better too. Sometimes I like that it takes time."

"Why couldn't we all of went?"

"Not a good idea."

"Are we against free speech?"

"What?"

"They're having this for free speech and Dudoo and Stanoodu are against them."

"We're not against free speech. We're against NAZIs"

"Everybody's against NAZIs. My mom specially."

"Everybody's against NAZIs except, apparently, NAZIs".

"So we should've went too. Did we have to stay here cuz we're girls?"

"We had to stay here because you're still a very young girl. You'd be in over your head."

"But they're not over theirs?"

"Yes, they are, but that's where grownups are most of the time. Don't give her that. That's not good for dogs. Go wash your hands please."

"If I wasn't here, you could've gone too. Would you want that?"

"After everything that's happened, nobody should have to go anywhere for this kind of horseshit. Our guys should've stayed home too because they're getting old. They should've stayed here in the air conditioning and watched the internet with us. You could learn a lot from your father."

"And Stan. Except when they talk stupid talk."

"Hmmph. You'll see plenty of young women out there too. And when you push in, use the heels of your hands. Like this."

"I sawed lots of old people last time. More old women than old men."

"This is different."

"Daddu says he hasta go cuz of me. And you hafta stay cuz of me. I'm sorry."

"Nothing is your fault. That's one sure thing."

"Don't be worried. My daddy won't let anybody hurt Stanush. There's nothin' to be scared of."

*

Thirty-Three

I've Been Waiting For So Long

"Will you let me read you this story?"

"That's my least favorite, Obby. Can't you read me another one?"

"But it's the one I want you to hear. And you know I had help from Stan and your Daddoo."

"Hmmph"

"Please, make me happy? I know you will read this when you get older, but I want so much for you to hear my voice when you do that. Can you let me read this?"

She didn't say anything. Sitting on the sofa, she leaned in and pushed her head against his shoulder. He wrapped an arm around her and she put a hand on his arm. She saw the numbers blurry through dark hairs, and she closed her eyes.

There wasn't always a wall.

He was sure of it.

When he was very young, there was no direction he could not go.

Every home was open. So was every heart. And there was food in every pot.

But as he got older he was pushed in certain ways, and it was impossible to go backward.

And when he was a little older than that, it was as if mighty winds were pushing him even in directions he would prefer not to go.

And then came the coldest, hardest, most blistering wind of all. It withered everything it did not flatten. It swept away everything it did not wither. It swept him to a place of fear and smell and darkness where friends were few and far between and where those few friends were quite likely to be withered, flattened, or swept away into mud or flames.

But then new worlds opened.

But even then, he could go some ways and not others.

Once you fall in love, you can never go back.
Once you have children, you can never go back.

There are many things that happen that cannot be undone.

Really nothing can be undone.

The winds, even when they do not blister, wither, or flatten, still push very hard. And as the years go by, they push harder and faster. Always forward. Never backward.

But memories can be faster than the fastest wind. This is true of good memories full of sweetness and fondness. Those made him want to slow down and think, even though they could make him very sad. And it is true of bad memories filled with bitterness, rage, fear, and blame. Those sometimes made him want to push on harder than the push of any wind, and even faster than memories which might try to catch up with him.

But you can never go faster than memories. Especially if you grow old. But maybe the wall was always there?

But what was behind the wall was not only memories though that was what he mistook them for at first. Because there were snatches of music and voices of laughter he had never heard before. There were whiffs of food he had never smelled before. There were faces and figures he had never seen before.

But there were also people he once knew. There were neighbors and friends. There were grandparents, aunts, cousins, and uncles. There were people he used to see whose names he never knew. And there were others he knew he had never met before: some of them strange and some strangely familiar.

But when they called out to him, or seemed to, they didn't always use his right name. And people he knew did not always recognize him or else they acted as if they thought he was someone else.

People he once knew and loved would say things they would never have said so long ago.

But all this happened when he was fairly old.

When he was young, he would rarely see the wall, much less encounter it. There might be glimpses through real or imaginary wilderness or between the clustered buildings in villages or towns or cities. Or there would only be faint wafts of sound, and he could never be truly sure where they came from.

But now that he was old, he often saw the wall. And when he could see the wall, he could also see the people, the fields, the trees, the animals, the villages, and the farms behind it. Now that he was old, he could often come right up to the wall and walk along its run. Sometimes beyond the wall, there was only thick forest or empty fields.

Other times there was a bright or misty meadow where he sometimes saw a girl with a red and white dress and a red and white hat. And sometimes she would smile shyly and sweetly when she saw him looking at her over the wall.

But the wall was not always the same. Sometimes it was old and irregular with stones fallen off. Or it could be so smooth and strong he could hardly see where each stone met.

Other times it was like the stones were moving and growing into and through each other; it was almost as if the wall were a living thing made of living things, unlike any living things he had ever thought of.

But even though the wall was never higher than his chest and usually not much higher than his waist, he could never climb over the wall.

The wind near the wall was always the same kind of strong.

It was like a breeze that was never too warm and never too cold. But if it was a wind that coursed *above* the wall, it was a very different kind of wind.

Above the wall was something like the wind except it made no noise. Like the wind, it could not be seen, but if he put out a finger it would turn it aside harder and faster than any worldly wind ever unfurled a flag. If he put out a hand, it would turn his whole frame aside in the direction it coursed like a rusty weathervane might be snapped just a quarter turn by a sudden gust from nowhere.

But no matter how forcefully it turned him aside, it never caused him pain or fright.

Eventually, no matter where he was, the wall was always nearby.

Eventually, he spent as much time looking at and over the wall as he spent wondering about the life around him, before him, or all the memories behind.

And then one day he could see that the wall which had once seemed mostly straight was now making sharper turns that seemed to block his way.

And since he could not climb over the wall, he'd turn in its new direction.

And every time this happened, he'd grow more weary and frail.

And then came a day where the wall made the sharpest turn of all.

And as he approached this new barrier, some of the stones, as if they were alive, moved down and aside to form a welcoming way.

And as he came closer to this beckoning breach, he could see people.

He could see people he knew and people he never knew. He could see his wife, the mother of his children. And she said, "I've been waiting for so long." He could see his mother and father. And they said, "We've been waiting for so long." He could see his brothers and sisters and his cousins, aunts and uncles. And they said, "We've been waiting so long."

He could see friends he knew as children, and he knew they were boys and girls who were never allowed to grow up. And they all said, "We've been waiting so long."

He could see his grandparents. He could see their great-grandparents. And farther in the distance were more and more people, here and there, stretching back farther than he could ever have seen before. And further than that were mountains. And further than that were oceans. And further than that were stars and swirling lights.

> **And everything seemed to say, "I've been waiting for so long."**

"What about animals, Obby? What about dogs and puppies? What about kitty cats and kittens? What about horsies, and bunnies, and chipmunks? What about them, Obby?"

*

Thirty-Four

Hydration Station

"Dat it? Gone already?"

"That's it! Cops just hustled them all into a van." Stan held his shaky friend's elbow, guiding him quietly toward tree shade.

"Adolf, we hardly knew ye!"

"Surely we couldn't hear ye. Maybe we could get a pizza and something to drink? OK, Abe?"

"I didn't see any NAZIs. Did you?"

"Fifty miserable little trimpulists?"

"Should've let 'em hadda mic. What they wanna speech free about anyways?"

"Guess you'll have to check'em out on YouTube."

"Right, Stan. But I been sweltering here. At least I stopped sweating."

Stan leaned in to catch Abe's words. "Ok, Abe. Goody. But let's just keep walking now."

"Pimply organizers said they weren't lettin no NAZI Klansmen speak. So whud they wanna say?"

"So. Ok. Abe! Let's go sit in the shade. Search *'Free Speech'*, *'Boston Common'*, *'Bandstand'.*"

"Wait! Dey gots water over there."

"I dunno Abe. They're pretty amped still."

"Yo! Hello!" Abe lurched toward the blackclads milling around a small portable table. "That water for anyone? Or jest the warrior class?"

"We're out of full small ones. Can I pour?" A young man in black tights held out a gallon jug and offered a clear empty pint.

"Oh. Why thank you. A gentleman and a scholar you are. Much appreciated."

"You don't have to pay." A young woman, also black-clad, smiled.

"Yeah. But. Here ya go. Oops!" Abe, recovering from a partial stumble, returned her pleasant smile as she handed back his fumbled wallet. "I dunno bout you, but I'm actually so so glad I didn't see no NAZIs."

"They were here though," said someone through a Jesse James mask.

"Well, so were you. And so were... how many overwhelming thousands? Overall a good day?"

From a lithe tree leaning desperado several dark paces away, "Hey didn't I see you on the bandstand?"

"Not me. Couldn't get near it. Wasn't allowed."

"So you tried to get in there."

"I was curious. They said..."

From a young Errol Flynn with flowing Robin Hood hair and Captain Blood goatee, "Are you a NAZI?"

"What's who?"

"Are you a fucking NAZI? It's a simple fucking question."

"It's an insulting fucking question…"

"You won't give a direct answer! That means you're a NAZI."

"Well, Seig Heil to you too. How can you say–"

"We don't talk to NAZIs!. Get the fuck outta here."

"And where should I go? Last I knew this was a public park here since Galileo last dropped a lead lump on his thumbtoe."

"Shut up! Get the fuck outta here. We're asking you nicely."

"Calling me a NAZI isn't 'nicely', strictly speaking."

"Shut the fuck up! Are you gonna go peacefully?"

"What gives you the right to tell me where to go in any literal sense?"

"NAZI! NAZI here! We gotta NAZI." One started as

others chorused. "NAZI here. NAZI over here!" More converged pointing, "NAZI! NAZI! *Get your red-hot NAZI! Get your ice-cold fascist!* Right here! NAZI!"

From a solemn, breathy covenmother came stern instruction, "I'm asking you to leave."

"Doncha see you're doing just what real NAZIs would do?"

From the spearpoint of an oncoming dark phalanx, "We don't take advice from NAZIs! Shut the fuck up!"

"How do you know I'm a NAZI? Just cuz this guy says so?"

"I trust him more than I'd trust a NAZI."

"Abey. Let's go! Thank you for the water."

"Wait a minute. I just found out I wuz a NAZI. Did you know that?"

"Abe! Let's go."

"Better listen to your friend, NAZI!"

"Outta here, NAZI!"

"Don't make us make you, NAZI!"

It took a dozen blackshirts, some wearing masks, to ring the hulking mass, and begin hustling him backward.

Amused, alarmed, indignant, and just ornery, Abe let his mass bulk down to the ground as forceful as a frictionless feather.

Passerbyers stopped passing by. Press members pressed in snapping shots and Ninjas pushed back to block them. Abe crawled awkwardly pursuing tossed glasses, deftly grasping them almost from under a dark warrior's fleet bootstep. Then, self-satisfied, he lay back to survey the surrounding melee in some semblance of blissful serenity.

"Abe! Abe! Are you alright? Can you get up? Abe?"

But round Avram Ider, now nearly one with the ages, was also one with the tumult. He was the cry and the crier, the scuff and the scuffler, the sky and the lier downer. A mature triplet of women wafted through the scrum and floated in close. One held out a hand to gentle Abe who sat up smiling to take it–though it took Stan and a few others, including one blackshirt, to hoist his heft onto unsteady feet.

Sunstruck and perplexed, he let himself be led to a shade-dappled bench.

"There wuzn't enough NAZIs so they had to make do!"

"Yup, Abe, I think you made their day!"

"To think I lived long enough to become Heil Hitler!"

"A shock trooper in a stupor. Abe, you don't look so good. Let's just rest a bit here."

"I'm a Riefenstahling Gary Cooper!" Abe's voice wavered between a croak and a gasp.

"Super Duper. Just sit."

"Wait! Wanna give them back their bottle!"

"What? Wait! No! Don't move, Abe!"

Waddling grey-faced, his vision clouding strangely, the weighty man propelled himself toward the encircled card table.

"Here! This yours!" he croaked before falling forward.

*

Thirty-Five

Check It Out

Uncle Stan just called from the Boston hospital. Daddusch fell down, but they're giving him a drip and he's gonna get better. Carol Ann says everybody's gotta take care of their health, their weight, and always drink enough water, not soda.

My dad acts like a dummy, but I know he cares for me even if it pees me off. Sometimes he makes me let him check what's in my pack like he did yesterday morning so I don't get scoliosis like Mrs. Kirshner. Now I only gots my boxes, my tablet, a bathing suit, a flip-flop because I lost one but it's somewhere, a towel, The Robe by Lloyd C. Dickless and Quo Vadis by Enrique Chinkavitz.

The night before Daddu Jewdoo said I wuz gettin to be a regular C-Moon Vile so we started singing it. Then I wisht we had a piano and someone who could plunk it but we just plugged in his smellphone and played it. And he did his Fat Daddy dance and I did my Cool Girl one.

And Paul McCartney really could be a proton because a proton can still be anywhere even when it's in a hydrogen that's in a water that's in a blood cell that's in a turtle that's in an ocean that's on a planet that's in a solar system that's in a galaxy that's in a cluster that's in a supercluster that's in in a universe that's in a turtle that's in another turtle that's in the mind of Ja, the turtle inside and outside all turtles.

That's in. That's out. That's in. And everything is always changing. And everything is always the same. And he doesn't have a mother so everybody has to love him.

What's it all to you?

*

memor rem suscipit

Home for the Jolly Days

Thirty-Seven

Transplant

She woke late to the grays, golds, and greens of a rainy autumn morning and, disturbing the dog, dragged her blanket, still draped over her shoulders, from the sofa.

Yawning Gracie stretched in her cushioned corner and blinked in annoyance before wagging in gentle acquiescence.

The TV was still on from the night before, its screen silent and blue.

She was hungry but, fixed by the wide window, she stood staring out at yellow leaves tossed up by winds or sweeping diagonally down from treetops. The misty light was just enough to glisten asphalt even where there were no rippling puddles.

It was not her home, but she could not leave. This living room, except for her nightly sofa nest, was kept tidy and organized by Carol Ann–who expected her to help.

Gretty strained to picture these shiny floors sticky with dustfuzzy spoons gummed to rumpled rugs. But here there were no coffee-stained newspapers or butterfingered magazines, no emptied yogurt containers half stuffed with socks or crumpled underwear. Barely noticed in her life long passed, such squalor, remembered now, provoked a piercing disdain that clashed with dulling thumps of grief.

It was not her home, but she had a bedroom here,

never used except for changing, with shelves and closets crammed with clothes and odd belongings. Carol Ann said it was a 'wonderful' place to bring friends and maybe have sleepovers. But there were no friends and, except for certain appointments, Gretty hadn't left the house since buried here the year before.

It was not her home, but Uncle Stan said it was her sheltering egg.

Off this enormous living room was an oversized closet, now 'her 'office,' with a desktop computer and its own humongous screen. She'd allowed Stan and Carol to coax her into online courses: Philosophy and Western Civilization before; C++ and PostPre-Calculus now. Carol Ann, easily frustrated with Math and allergic to programming, needed gentle tutoring. Uncle Stan, prone to nervous explosions whenever a point failed to get easily across, frequently provoked Carol's loud remonstrations. But such din could be easily switched off if ever it failed to enliven the process of learning.

It was slowly dawning she might already know more about Maths and coding than Uncle Stan, but she was quite confident in her ability to help him keep up.

Stan wanted R.I.T. "So much money for deaf people!", he'd say, and she could "make friends!"

Sure.

Carol Ann wanted The Elms. If that was too Catholic, Smith or Mt. Holyoke were also nearby. Very strangely, Carol Ann had no disdain for girl schools. "What is wrong with you?" she'd loudly bray to Stan. "Maybe she needs the security of staying close to home."

She wasn't home, and college was years away.

"But maybe by then, this will be home for you," Carol would insist.

Maybe then. Maybe then. Maybe by then, anything could happen. Maybe.

In the kitchen she toasted an English muffin and made hot chocolate, sneaking in a spoon of instant coffee. Carol's car was gone, probably to the farm market. Stan, most likely, was sleeping upstairs or propped in bed with Marbles and a laptop. She felt momentarily tempted to step outside and let her face feel cool mist. But after breakfast, she simply tidied up and leapt back to her sofa for snuggles with Gracie and breathing bad dog breath.

> *It was not fire. It was not ice.*
> *The storm inside was not electric*

in any common sense. There were no sharp bursting flashes, only a roiling that wrinkled more than air. It curdled even rigid things with crinkles, folds, and dark fractures, spreading and contracting, doing what an ungentle lava lamp might do to a landscape half-skyed. But the jarring displacement felt more like words that could not fit together except for sometimes in strangely smoky, scattered, fleeting, maddening ways.

Then it was gone. She sat up blinking and with an ache in her jaw.

Her dad had said gravity was the force pulling everything together while grace splayed everything far apart. Another name for grace is entropy. These were not about 'up' or 'down' because those meant something only to someone still stuck on a planet–which he was not anymore.

Uncle Stan said it was "just the suppository". Grace didn't pull things apart. It shrunk them at speeds faster than light, tricking physicists into empty searches for dark energy. Gravity kept everything we'll ever know still swirling while entropy engendered additional dimensions and entirely new universes everywhere and all at once.

Gravity was what felt like love still trying to keep them close while entropy dragged her father fast away, thinning him and making him vapory like smoke rising higher and higher, twisting from a thick column to a wispy veil to a distant shimmer. It had been that way with her mom—only harsher and more wrenching—like her. That was how the fat dad explained dead-mom feelings to her then, but now was now. And grace and gravity kept everything clashing and swirling just as they forged and troubled the earth, everything on it, all known galaxies, and even her own self, shelled in this tiny corner of time and space.

It was not her home, but they'd pretty much surrendered to her three rooms: the office closet Carol rarely tidied even though Gretel never had, a bedroom where she perched her parents' unmixed ashes, and this living room—and not only at nights. Here, a reading corner was sectioned off by a loveseat, a rocker, an armchair, and some lamps. Aside from a small window, this corner's wallspans were bookshelved with over a quarter of their stackspace emptied for her and already half filled with her own library and other books from home. Anne Frank was there. So was Temple Grandin and Malala. There was a book of cave art, books full of photographs, and one with only Picassos. Charles Dickens was there with his *Child's History of England,* Ebenezer Scrooge, and *Great Expectations.* She had *Of Mice and Men, In Dubious Battle, To Kill a Mockingbird, The Persian Boy,* and *Catcher in the Rye.*

Portrait of the Artist as a Young Man sat half-read there. There were Uncle Wigglies, Dr. Dolittles, a full set of Mary Poppins, half the OZ series, and all but the last Harry Potter. There was the Children's Illustrated Bible, once Carol's, now hers. There was her mother's genocide book. There was Charles Lamb. There were some books on autism and one about American Sign Language. There were the old MAD magazines scrounged by her father, all his Beatle and Coltrane books, and a Kinkos bound manuscript of his entitled "A Book Jew Dreams of Money."

All the Beatles CDs were there, and most of Robyn Hitchcock's. There was every CD her father ever burned her including one he'd labeled "Punny Songs by Bobby Zimm". But not all those made her laugh. He'd slipped in two versions of "Forever Young" with

"You're Gonna Make Me Lonesome When You Go". He'd said it was for when she grew up and left him old so she'd keep in touch and visit. She'd said he was already old, and he'd said that was her fault.

Maybe everything was.

Nobody stays forever young, and maybe that was a good thing if she were to believe what people had told her since her mother quit. They'd say stuff tended to get better. Of course, some admitted that same stuff might first get worse as she moved through her teens. She'd learned about part of that one evening in the bathroom the stormy night her dad had to bash in the door.

Despite stray pangs, she'd always known many ways she was better off without her mom. Maybe it wasn't so strange her father-grief stayed mostly inside when mudder grief had always seemed, even to her, so much like a show. But, on her own, she hadn't left this property, which was not really hers, since moving in to stay. For now.

Nobody remains forever young, and maybe things do 'get better' as you age. But why would any good person want ever to have a child? How could they witness it exposed to all this even when they didn't croak first? Carol Ann said God sent children to their chosen parents, but Carol Ann, who took nobody else's bull-shit, could always bullshit herself. It was all so sternly confirmed by books given her after the bloody bath-room incident. Everything was so horrible and more disgusting than she'd ever imagined. It was better to be-lieve in no God than one who'd contrived stuff so ugly and alarming.

Gretty loved boys in photos, movies, books, and dreams. But she knew, really, they'd want to put her with a baby. And if hers were a girl? There'd be no ghastly way to protect such a one from its own ghastly insides. Maybe this explained her own gone mom, always so brittle and distant. Sometimes she even cried for the dried and jagged mud she'd carried a year on her back.

But a boy from her might be all right, a boy who just took what he needed and didn't care. And until she died, with hooded eyes she'd hover like a hawk to help him make his way.

*

Thirty-Eight

Money Shiva

I knew it was something right away. I knew by how she listened so stiff. That's not how she usually is on the phone.

Carol Ann's like everybody else, different depending on who she's talking to. She's nowhere near as triple faced as my Mudd was or even me, but still. One phone voice is her "giving advice" one. That's her best because she always has to be helping. Another is her fake happy girly voice for women she doesn't like, but who likes women anyway? There's also her "Take Us Off Your List!" voice which doesn't even ever work. HA!

Mostly Carol's all bossy pants feminazi acting like Stan's all schlub, so it's really not a good sign if she gives up the phone to him like that.

Anyway, it was a lawyer who'd got the number from Anty calling about Zeyde-Izzy who was dying.

I hadn't seen Z since dad's memorial. Back then I was still carrying Mudd's white crushed-up bones in my backpack. That's when he gave me those two boxes. "For whatever you want," he said. But I knew he knew what they were for.

They're both wood and about the same size. One looks old. It has brass corners, brass hinges, and a brass wrapping band that's lined with rows of tiny carved-in decorations. The other's more modern. It's squarer, made of two different woods curved together to make designs like eyes or some strange ancient picture alphabet.

I keep them upstairs.

I never knew what to say to Z so I just said thank you. All he did was touch my hair and walk away, not even staying for food. It felt kind of bad when he left, like I should have said something.

Now he wanted to tell me about Benny before he croaked.

Bennie's my uncle because he's my Mudd's brother which means he's a BLOOD uncle, unlike Nuncle Stan who's no real relation at all. But if he and Carol take care of me now, I can take care of Bennie later–because Bennie can't take care of himself and won't ever be able to.

I knew all about this already even before we got to his hospital, which was right near Central Park.

I went with Carol Ann this time. She will NOT drive into Boston, or Cape Cod, or That City so we parked in New Haven and took the train.

It was a grey city day.

This hospital seemed taller and smaller than Mass General was. Z's room was practically on the top floor and Bennie was there already. That was sad because I knew he was going to be an orphan like me now. Someone from his Home was there too. She was all dressed in leather, and I didn't like that and watched her like a hawk. After a while, I saw she wasn't so tough, but I don't like that either.

Benny can't take care of himself.

GrampaZ knew it was me because he grabbed my hand, and said "Good girl" and "Bennie". That's all he said except for "You stay," and "Be good." but he must've said it three dozen times. "Good girl." "Bennie."

I understood the first time.

And then there was nothing to do.

The TV was always on. Leather Girl had earphones. I had my iPad. Carol had her iPhone. Nurses busted in and out, and once I laughed because I thought of Catch-22 and the man in white plaster.

I never knew Z had so many people working for him, but they kept on coming. Some lawyers, some assistants, and some whatevers. They wanted us to stay at Z's, but Carol didn't wanna agree so we almost stayed in a hotel. Leather Girl took Bennie home every night, but somebody's assistant drove them both back and forth.

Turns out we could just walk to Z's so that's where we slept.

It took a few days. I saw his feet turn blue, but I never heard any rattle. His face just got grayer and grayer, and when his breathing got hoarse they pumped more Fentanyl. His last breath was all alone one night. There weren't any machines that went BEEP, and no line to watch go flat.

He said something before we left that day before his last night. He said, "I get stronger. Only stronger all the time. And now." I think that's what he said, but he was dying. I only thought he might be talking about me except then he said in a squeaky hoarse wheeze, "Don't get so strong too quick. You."

The service was the next day so Stan drove down. Lots of people came, but I think they were mostly there on business because of how they talked outside the room. At the graveyard, it was almost just us.

Anti said I could sit Shiva if I was going to insist. So did Portnoy, the lawyer. Carol wasn't happy but didn't know what to say. She had to get back to work. "Poor kid," Stanislaw always says. "Part of the 99%." Boy, that makes her mad!

Anyway, if Bennie was going to sit Shiva, so was I. It wasn't going to be just him and Leather Girl.

I thought Shiva would be more boring than it was. First of all, Z lived upstairs in a cool building with a doorman. The lobby, the corridors, and the elevator were all pretty fancy. Stan said, "Swanky". And Z's housekeeper was still there. She was a nice Polish woman who couldn't speak English much, but seemed happy when everybody always had a plate or a glass or a cup that didn't need filling.

Interesting people dropped by. Some only stayed for coffee or else just a little slug. Stan didn't know how kosher that was, but then he said lots of those mugs weren't all that kosher either so what the hell.

Benny wouldn't sit on the box even after I put a couch cushion on it. He kept going up on the couch. I only sat on the box for a while too, so I didn't blame him. Me and hims played lots of Monopoly with Leather Girl. He needed help with that, but not with checkers. He almost beat me once at checkers for real, but I mostly let him win every other game. Leather Girl always let him win. Faker.

I looked it up and saw Shiva actually means seven. Stan said that wasn't HIS fault, and I said it wasn't mine either. Like I'm going to be stuck there THAT long? But eventually, I decided Benny wasn't going to mind one way or the other so why should I? BE-SIDES if I was going to be a ZEALOT about it, I'd have to make him sit on a WOODEN box for the whole time. And I'd have to too in a pig's eye. Anyway, it really wasn't up to us.

I found out Helen, the housekeeper, was getting paid for the whole month—even after we left. Her moving costs would be paid for too. Maybe this was because of Z, or maybe it was Portnoy. Portnoy's the executor lawyer who's like a very cute boy with a very good brain. Either way, it's a good thing (MITZVAH!) and I liked how he smiled when I told him that. And I don't care whose money people use when they do good things.

Stanley said it was kind of a "money shiva" because it was. Ever since my dad died, I notice Stan uses lots more Jewish words which is weird because he's not even Jewish and neither is Carol, but I'm glad he taught me "mitzvah".

Z hired guardians for me and Bennie. Bennie also gets an extra one from the state. We have a trust fund for him, and I need to help run it when I'm 18.

I was always pretty nice when Z was around because he was a little scary. But I kind of wish I could tell him off now because he was "ESPECIALLY AND REPEATEDLY EXPLICIT" in the goddamn paperwork, that I get NOTHING unless I "CONSISTENTLY AND DILIGENTLY ENDEAVOR TO ENSURE" Bennie has "THE BEST AND MOST PROPER CARE PRESENT AND AVAILABLE AT ALL TIMES"!

Portnoy had to repeat this kind of stuff again and again and AGAIN to make sure I understood. I INDUBITABLY would've gotten even more wicked pissed off if I didn't see he was kind of embarrassed, and I told him so. I said I'd do those things for Bennie the best I could EVEN if there wasn't any frigging money at all. Not everybody has money! Do their handicapped relatives get dumped in the street? The whole thing still makes me bounce up and down whether I'm sitting or standing. Even if I'm lying down, it jerks me up like a jolty vampire sometimes.

Zeyde-Z just liked everything double and triple-checked. That's *what Portnoy said. His real name is Jason Roth, but Stan thinks Portnoy's funnier.*

It must be a bad world. So many people got good reasons not to trust anybody.

But Portnoy touched my tight fist. And when I held my hand up, he just touched my palm with two light fingertips. I couldn't even look back at his sad eyes because I was too afraid I'd snot cry. (Well I did. But only into my hands after I twisted away from him.)

There was way more money stuff I can't even remember. I don't really need to know any of it until I'm 18. Turns out Bennie's my only relative on my mudder's side. My cousins and Anti are only on my dad's side. Of course, doof COULD'VE knocked somebody up when he was a boy. That might be fun to have a half-brother or sister.

I'm pretty sure Bennie will never got a baby—unless some chick rapes him, but that wouldn't be the baby's fault and it would be my first cousin too. My two now cousins did come, but only for an hour. Anti Sheila took them home after they started a pillow fight with the couch cushions. And she apologized with wet eyes TO ME!

It was mostly fun being with Bennie, trying to see how he saw things. He wasn't too sad about his father, my shriveled old Zeyde-Z. I even TRIED to make him cry, but even after I told him again and again how he'd never see the miserable old stiff again, never ride in his car again, never get ice cream with him again, he just got quiet. Maybe because he could tell I was being a bitch. Maybe it was the ice cream.

I was mostly nice though, and it was more fun to make him

smile than cry like the first day when Helen made chicken soup. Whenever anyone said "Chicken Soup", Bennie would say "Can't hoit!" which was not funny except for how he smiled afterward.

Some things aren't ever funny, and even hilarious stuff can get annoying after too many times. But Bennie didn't do it on his own. Somebody else had to say "Chicken Soup" first, and it just got funnier and funnier. Even Leather Girl got giggling and said "Chicken Soup" a few times. It didn't matter what you were talking about, but it had to be the first thing or last thing you said.

If you said "Chicken Soup is better hot," he'd say "Can't hoit!"

If you said, "Chicken Soup, bumble bee, dirty knickers, and yellow bandana," he'd say "Can't hoit!"

If you said, "Four score and eleven years ago, our Father who aren't in chicken soup," he'd say it.

If you whispered it, he'd say "Can't hoit!" just as loud as always. If you sang it like, "My baby likes to poop in chieey kaann souuuuppah!", he'd still say it regular.

But if you said, "A little girl took a whittle whirl and got bit by a squirrel while eating chicken soup with a whip cream swirl that made her hurl," he wouldn't —unless you STOPPED after "chicken soup."

He wouldn't say it if you just said "chicken" or just said "soup", but would if you said "chicken poop" or "slick and goop" or "dick and loop" or "fricken scoop" or "prick and droop" which would've made Leather Girl spurt milk out her nose if she was drinking some. I wish!

He never got tired of it, but it's the kind of thing that goes *from being funny, then not funny, and then even more funnier than ever.*

But there was something else.

One night I found a packet of newspapers and magazines in Z's desk. The first page I unfolded had little pictures of Obby, Z, and Mudd. I'd seen those pictures a bunch of times, but not all together and not in newspapers.

I already knew Z was in a German camp like Obby was too. It might have been the first real thing I ever knew. Both of them were lucky not to get ovened.

The problem was someone found out Z helped the NAZIs. That was a real big deal especially for my sputtering mudder even though Z'd always given hunks of money to tons of Jewish groups. His office had pictures of him with all the famous Israelites. I know who was Golda Meyer and freakn' Bibi. I learned about cool guy Moshe Dayan, David Ben Gurian, and a few others.

I always knew Z'd even paid for Mudd and Obby to go to libraries and auditoriums all over the place so Obby could help her sell her stupid books. That was when I first started staying with Carol and Stan. But the whole point was Germans had done bad things to all the Jewish people, but now it turns out some Jews helped them and did bad things too. And Z was one of them. This all happened a long time ago, but it was a real big SCANDAL in a lot of newspapers anyway.

So that whole thing ended up making my mess of a nutty Mudder look like an asshole in front of every Jew in the whole wide world because she'd written all about Obby, but also about

Z like they were BOTH only victims. Maybe someday I'll write a book about "My Full of Shit Shit-talking Crazy Clown Mom" and I'll be famous.

Z wasn't nice like Obby, and we hardly saw him. But I think sometimes he did want to be more friendly but just didn't know how. Like me. So maybe I'll never learn either.

Z was a dried-out old zombie who smacked around starving captives when he was young and juicy. Mudd was a mean lump of misery even when her hair wasn't on fire. Daddu was a goofy fat slob who scared people by being too loud and crazy. And his Abba, my Obby, was so shy and quiet, nobody'd ever notice him if they didn't get a chance to hear what he could say.

I guess it doesn't look too good for me.

On the other hand, what makes anybody any better?

If Z didn't help the Nazis, they'd just've murdered him. And if they killed Z, I'd never been born. Doesn't that make me cursed? My mudder too?

Probably.

I'm not sure things get better because the more I know, the worse everything seems.

Stanly said something interesting though. When black people were slaves down south, even good moms made sure to "whup" their children good. But that was really to protect them because white people could beat them to death or burn them alive—or all kinds of wicked bad shit. So whatever Z did to other Jews, it wasn't as bad as the Nazis doing what they did. I guess Nazis are the worst kind of white people.

But it doesn't mean Z never saved anyone but himself.

I'm getting so I don't know what's good and what's bad anymore.

It's like they're all small black balloons. My mudder, my fudder, Obby, and even Z. I can't see them anymore because they're so up and lost in grey far clouds. But their strings are tied into me and I feel their tugs. Only I can't pull them back, and I can't cut the strings.

I'd only want to pull back Obby and maybe Daddu.

Carol Ann would say it's just selfish to think too much about this kind of stuff. It might be misery for me, but so many people are way more worse off. So many people live and die scared all the time, always being whipped or tortured or starved. And they never even know why.

They'd love to live here where there's streetlights, libraries, ice cream shops, fireplaces, and happy dogs who wriggle when they see you coming. I could go outside in the snow right now and not be cold because I have good boots and warm clothes.

Then there's all these tons of extra money they got for me. Sounds like I only need to make sure Bennie stays happy and safe. All he needs is clean clothes, good food, a warm bed, and somebody to say "Chicken Soup" once in a while.

I should be happy.

* * *

Oh, and Z said something else too. I almost forgot it because it makes no sense, but that's why I remember it too. He said, "There is no time."

Thirty-Nine

The Weaver of Baghdad

Streamly Gredible lay still drowsy on her couch. With one hand pressed beneath her waistband, she stretched a dainty foot into the silky fur of a snickering cur who moistened the dry spaces between her toes with a snaking tongue while also cooling nicely their tips with a friendly nose.

Then her grabby hand slipped into a slippery stack of improvised preprints resting half spread on the floor. Pulling up one booklet, she set it atop her mound of blankets and propped herself with pillows to peruse it in the draping sunlight of a morning that fell heavily into the room through a wide window which could have pictured a tree cathedraled street had the girl any inclination to peer out at even the most sheltering of vistas.

It was a manuscript half crafted by her old Obby back when there were still laps to sit on. Now, self-cuddled in someone else's home, she heard again her younger self incessantly interrupt with pressured questions. But also, fondly, she felt the memory of a gentle grayed head push heavily against her stressed impatience.

Who was Shahrazad? Why did she tell so many stories? Why did the Sultan kill his wives? Why did he like stories? Which was his favorite? Where is Baghdad? Have you been there? Can we go? Was she pretty? Was he handsome? Was he old? Which one of the thousand and one was this? Why do you think it's so funny? I never heard of ANY Richard Burton! Don't you think your own are better? Why is Dadoo cackling like that?

Her father could still roost in a corner of a couch to watch and wisecrack. And she could still crack back.

This one was *The Weaver of Baghdad*. But Baghdad was not about fathers, nor was it about bags. It was, and is, a city of many streets, many markets, and many stories. And what weavers do is tighten long lines of thread together and make wide webs of flat fabrics. Grandfathers, fathers, and daughters are like fibers extending all the way back through monkeys to slime molds. So are grandmothers, mudders, and sons.

Through such strands are passed many others. One is the warp. The other is the "woof woof", which is whatever happens to fathers and daughters while they live including whatever they do to each other while being stretched down toward new grandbabies.

And again, she reread with the old voice in her head.

The slave girl Shahrazad massaged the Sultan's youthful foot through its silky slipper. He frowned down upon her while sipping uneasily from his chalice of fortified wine.

"That's enough bloody Sinbad for now. How 'bout one with a genie?"

"Genies are not the only masters of magic, my Sire," smiled Shahrazad in a way proven to soothe the fiercest truculence of boy kings. "In my heart, tonight is a story passed on to this day by a line of Viziers rightly renowned for their sage counsel to the mightiest kings, emperors, caliphs, and sultans."

"Humph," grumbled the callow Sultan, "Sometimes I wonder about your esteemed Vizier. Crafty he may be. And wise in his own way. But am I the primary beneficiary of his many wiles?"

"Consider, O my Master, this story of 'The Weaver of Baghdad' and judge for thyself whether or not it has come from one who has nothing but devotion to the natural order that sets some men above others and each man above all the women who must bear them—and you, Most Potent One, above all but the Carapaced Creators."

"Very well," sighed the Sultan, lifting his head so he might lay it upon her tender loins once she had couched beside him. "I suppose you, by now, must know what I like."

"It begins, My Lord, thusly," purred the storyteller as her sovereign closed his eyes and hastened to comfort himself.

The Weaver of Baghdad

"O harken thee, O Ruler of the World, to a tale of one who once resided under the beneficence of thy forefathers and who was ever an exemplar of the most wondrous ingenuity ever to flourish thanks to the just rule of a dreadful monarch. And relish also the stupendous folly lurking always in low-born hearts, forever awaiting opportunity to overthrow the well-being of even the worthiest of commoners, all of whom would be completely undone if not for the firm laws and sagacious mercies of a wise ruler, divinely ordained.

"Furthermore, O Spurting Fountain of Lavish Boons, congratulate thyself upon the notion that even the most base and shameful comportment of the guilty may, under the blessings of noble oversight, become memorable lessons to promote stirrings of purity even among the coarsest and most debauched of women and men.

"For the object of this tale is a low-born man who was from birth regarded a simpleton though his brother had risen by merit to the rank of Vizier whose single pleasure and purpose in every waking moment of life was to ensure his Sultan's word was heard and obeyed in every corner of the realm and that no mischief or happenstance could compound so as to trouble the tranquility of the Sultan's mighty sway.

"Know thee also this churl was a hunchback, as ill-favored of face and form as he was derelict of reason, and that the Vizier, his brother, was moved by considerations of propriety to sequester him to an upper story of his humble abode so he might ply his craft as a weaver of fine carpets and tapestries without otherwise troubling the sensibilities of the decent and the just.

"And for many years this weaver, a prattler whose name was Al Bak Buk, remained confined safely and, despite his mental deficiencies, grew ever more skillful in his chosen craft.  In his secluded tower, he produced ever finer cloths and fabrics incorporating scenes and patterns of much vividness and intrigue. Know Thee also that many of his contrivances were of a such so as to delight and inspire wonder among the young, the old, the base, and the highborn.

"And be well aware how products of this weaver's skill were of such fine quality, their pleasing patterns were rightly judged to merit admiration in the luxurious apartments of the Vizier, the houses of the wealthiest landowners–and of the most discerning merchants who, from time to time, garnered rich profits by selling them to far-flung buyers whether they were fierce sheiks of the desert, castled marauders among the Franks, Jewish bankers of the Adriatic, or serene potentates among the inscrutable Chinese. Even the palace walls and floors of the Grand Sultan himself were not disgraced to display the pick of this base villain's alluring handicrafts.

"And be additionally aware how some of the depictions insinuated into this miscreant's designs were of a particular nature such that refined men of exquisite taste felt free to enjoy them only in closeted privacy and to share them rarely and discreetly with none but their most worthy intimates or trusted concubines. Then carefully appreciate and consider how frequently it was the case that the Vizier felt honorably compelled to consign certain shocking products of his lamentable brother's loom to an all-consuming fire lest they bring infamy and condemnation upon his house due to the sordid and shameful nature of the imagery imposed upon them by the incorrigible craftsman.

"Now it was so there was but one window in the closed tower where the weaver worked with all varieties of silks, linens, hemps, sisals, jutes, and every type of wool known to mankind. And on warm days this misshapen hunchback was known to thrust his head and shoulders out under the wide-open sky so as to enjoin a mellifluous breeze to ruffle through his scruffy beard, to follow with his beady eyes the flights of birds whether they be raptors, prey, or carrion eaters, and also to espy the myriad happenings on the jostling street below.

"And one spring afternoon when this wretched knave was so extended whilst picking his teeth and flicking the detritus onto awaiting cobblestones and the heads of those who trod unwittingly upon them, he happened to perceive the toothsome wrists and alabaster forehead of a maiden fair as the moon while she watered wanton flowers in a window box across the way. And with his sly eyes, he observed the shy orbs of the damsel widen and her veiled face whiten as she apprehended his appreciation before hastily pulling closed the shutters to shield her modesty against his importunity.

"And so weeks passed. And then months. And over such expanse of days and hours, it became less uncommon for this rascal to encounter myriad enchanting apparitions of pulchritude and virginity framed in the merry window across the way. And the star-crossed weaver became, in this way, ever more prone to neglect his loom in his anxiety to avoid losing any opportunity of exchanging tempting glances with the delightful visions that presented themselves to him thusly at unexpected intervals and eventualities.

"And although this reprehensible scamp was confirmably dim-witted, it gradually occurred to him there was more than a single lone lady who would but occasionally grace his vantage in the enchanted window so near - and yet so inaccessibly distant to any of his innumerable shortcomings and unmentionable proclivities.

"Now it came to pass that a neighborhood washer-woman and flower seller was once persuaded to convey a message to this miserable little toiler via a maidservant who abided in his brother's house. This missive was penned by the young mistress of a bevy of lithesome enchantresses

who dwelled in the building across the way. She represented herself as the only daughter of a powerful merchant who endured the majority of her life confined to the uppermost apartments of her sire's fine townhouse. Though they were quite adept at devising their own entertainments, the note explained, they had of late become much distracted by the prospect of such a fine and noble gentleman whom they frequently perceived in the opposite window. He was, they were assured, a man of much accomplishment and pleasant mien who might certainly brighten some of their hours with learned and witty discourse while beguiling them with his mature charms and virile dignity if only the means could be found to gain him admittance to their luxurious, but too sterile, abode. And now, after much fretting and anxious strategizing, a means had presented itself to them in the form of a washerwoman who had access to both their houses. Therefore, they obsequiously begged him to make himself ready and available for the instant when this plan might be executed - which, they assured him, would occur quite presently or in the immediate, and none-too-distant, future.

"As anyone with the slightest powers of cognition might imagine, this deplorable toiler was soon sorely overcome with agitation and anticipation at such an improper prospect - and from that moment was in such a state he could rightly be described as veritably quivering with outlandish ideas and longings.

"And before two moons had risen and set in the dark

night skies overarching the venerable city of Baghdad, a servant girl of his brother, accompanied by the washer-woman and two giggling maidens, appeared at the threshold of his apartment and bade him to contort himself into a capacious laundry basket by which they proposed to bear him to his much-awaited assignation across the way. Upon compressing himself into the bottom of the wicker cradle, this doltish halfwit was to his dismay forthwith buried under a profusion of soiled linens and undergarments that fairly suffocated him with their noisome emanations.

"So already gagging and retching from the stench of such unimaginably intimate aromas, this abject blockhead then found himself being roughly bounced, jolted, and thumped against the steps and walls of countless stair-wells as the handmaidens failed to gently lift the basket but instead bashed it violently all about with scarce regard for his comfort or safety. And as the entirety of what might have cushioned his head and tailbone was stuffed above rather than wedged between his flesh and the hard bottom of the coffin, he was compelled to suffer many painful bumps and bruises during this ill-fated expedition.

"After an excruciating journey during which bone-jarring collisions prevented the foul reek of stained unmentionables from causing him to swoon into oblivion, this contemptible good for nothing was cast into the midst of an enticing assemblage of comely vixens all clapping and gasping in merriment as he staggered to his feet and attempted to present to them a dignified greeting.

"They bade him sit on a teetering stack of folded carpets and served him many sweetmeats and fortified wines as they sang spritely melodies at first as chaste as they were mellifluous. Then, as they plied him with more intoxicating concoctions, they began to dance and sway in an increasingly alluring manner as the types of ballads they performed grew ever more lusty until achieving a level of wantonness that might inspire blushes of discomfort in all but the most licentious of brothels.

"Eventually they coaxed him to join into their spirit of Terpsichore, and soon he found himself being swayed nearly off his feet and dizzyingly pirouetted as each fleet-footed nymph took turns hurling him from one to the other. But from time to very unexpected time one of the nubile merrymakers would soon box him quite sharply on his ear which would make him groan and see stars such that his knees were fain to buckle.

"But on each such occasion, the entire company of lovelies would swarm around him with profuse apologiesand dramatic expressions of comforting concern before enticing him to reluctantly recommence their strenuous festivities. However, there came a time when their buffets against his ears became so frequent and their blows to the nape of his neck so energetic that the hapless oaf was, at last, knocked senseless.

"Still, when the worthless miscreant was awakened to the dulcet airs of lutes and finger cymbals along with the luxurious sensations of having his temples and wrists massaged with fragrant oils while his feet were rubbed and kneaded by sinuous hands that held them tightly upon sturdy thighs, he ludicrously allowed himself to be lured into depths of folly even more profound than those into which he had heretofore descended.

"A slave girl escorted him to an adjoining closet whispering in his ear that he had won the high regard of her noble mistress, a lady of grand estate and voluptuous desires. All that need be done now, she explained, was to allow his eyebrows to be plucked and for her to shave

clean his chin and upper lip. Reassured this would enable the exquisite target of his lust to enjoy him as if he
were a smooth-cheeked boy, he shamefully agreed to
such an infamy.

"When he was returned to the larger company, not only
shorn and plucked, but rouged and powdered like the
crudest of strumpets, the ladies and their maidservants
were so overcome with merriment they could not
forbear from pelting his empty head with pillows, fans,
and powder puffs as well as with oranges, citrons,
tamarinds, avocados, guavas, olives, papayas, lychees,
date plums, grapefruits, figs, and pineapples until this
prince of dunces once again collapsed into moan heaving unconsciousness.

"He regained what remained of his wits to the solicitous
coos and soothing murmurs of a hovering coven of
seeming well-wishers who bade him only to don the
female attire of a dancing girl so that he might attain his
unworthy end of dallying with the mistress of the
household until the morning crow. Thusly was he
persuaded to abase himself with the tawdry additions of
anklets and bracelets spangled with jangling bells. And
with all their wit and wiles they coached him to master
all manner of steps and hi-jinx, whirls and undulations,
twirls and twerks until they propelled him to the center

of the floor with much slapping on the nape of his neck. And thusly was his doom sealed.

"For in the midst of this fool's gamboling, prancing, capering, and shoop-shoop shim-shimming about, the Master of the House who had surreptitiously returned to be rudely disturbed by an unseemly din in the upper chambers of his house burst onto this scandalous scene to the panicked shrieks and pitiful moans of the entire feminine company who..."

"And now my dear sovereign," purred the lovely Shahrazad with a tenderness such as would endlessly reverberate in the memories of the young Sultan whose head still rested upon her pillowy lap, "I fear the completion of this tale must await our next assignation on the morrow night. That is, O Lord of Earth and Stars, unless you find the crude lascivity of this particular yarn too low and sordid for thy refined predilections?"

The Sultan smiled in response and, like a sleepy pup, wriggled comfortably into the cushions of his bedstead and the softness of his bedmate. "O Baby," he sighed "You knoooow what I like!"

The next day proceeded like any other. The Sultan hunted with falcons, swam with the companions of his youth, played chess with a visiting ambassador, pardoned some petty forgers, scolded a philanderer, read a few petitions, and signed a proclamation or two. His Vizier, while receiving constant reports from deputies, eunuchs, guards, concubines, and hirelings all assuring him the Sultan's activities unfolded in an orderly and seemly manner, also conducted his usual number of confidential meetings with all manner of officials, officers, dignitaries, emissaries, spies, and subordinates. One of those meetings was with Shahrazad who had, in the passing months, become an ever more frequent confidant.

That evening, after night had fallen and banqueting had concluded, Shahrazad made her accustomed way to the royal apartments. She passed through three sets of gilded doors each guarded by a pair of armed soldiers handpicked by the Vizier. She ensured the attendants had well prepared the royal bath and that his most skillful masseuse was present for when her Lord should emerge from the perfumed waters. She confirmed the flowers were all fresh and fragrant and that the lutists, flutists, and choristers were well-rehearsed and discreetly positioned behind decorous blinds.

And when the freshly bathed young Sultan was stretched on the massage table and she had commenced feeding him the pink grapes which were his favorite, she braced herself for the fast rush of armed men who dashed in nearly noiselessly to seize their lawful sovereign. And after they had roughly bound him and put out his eyes, she remained to endure his shrieks of pain and rage and fear to tend and bandage his agonizing wounds.

And for decades after the old Vizier had fulfilled his promise of installing her as the first concubine of the new Sultan, a man of many conquests and victories, Shahrazad would daily frequent the small apartment of the former Sultan, now a blinded captive, and comfort him with stories of princes, and virgins, and sailors, and barbers, and tailors, and thieves, and prostitutes, and genies, and sea monsters, and young girls taken captive by fierce soldiers riding horses with wings.

* * *

Greta let the manuscript flop on her lap; sensations from its story swarming, unresolved, through and around her. But soon another image interposed and would not be brushed away; the blotchy blue-black marks on Zeyde Obby's old man's arm.

Many times, reading, resting, sitting at breakfast, walking in the sun, riding in a car, or wilting in front of a TV's bright blare, she'd run a finger over those tattoos. When done in silence, he'd merely grunt or sigh in his quiet Obby way. Maybe he'd pet her hair or kiss lightly her forehead. Asking out loud, a rare event, would prompt a solemn gathering of himself, a preparation for a story he'd told many times in the work of his old age, but never effectively to her.

Any vague allusion he might have conveyed to her regarding his tempest-tossed role in history's grand sweeps were now subsumed into a vaster and more vivid flow of stories now associated with Carol's Illustrated Bible. The same was so for Obby's few furtive references to wrenching personal details of loss, terror, deprivation, or triumph. Captivity, slavery, murder, deliverance, and revenge were all interchangeable patterns to be woven into and out of other strands of nurturance, romance, and blissful oblivion.

Whatever he didn't say, attention to his scar-marked arm always caused Obby to pull into himself in ways that made him grow greater. It added a layer of gentle over the solidity of his determination. But her other grandfather was different.

Noticing Zeyde-Z's tattoo would get his gaunt old face even sharper and ever more hollow. His frame would stretch until gallows-like he'd overarch any inquiry. His eyes would narrow. His mouth would extend in a grinning 'O' like a wolf that just might howl-or lunge.

Greta with a naked toe thrice tapped Gracie's cool wet

nose, and the silky doggie snickered again before wolf-
ishly leaping up to lick her salty face.

*

Forty

What I Don't Know Alone, I'll Never Forget

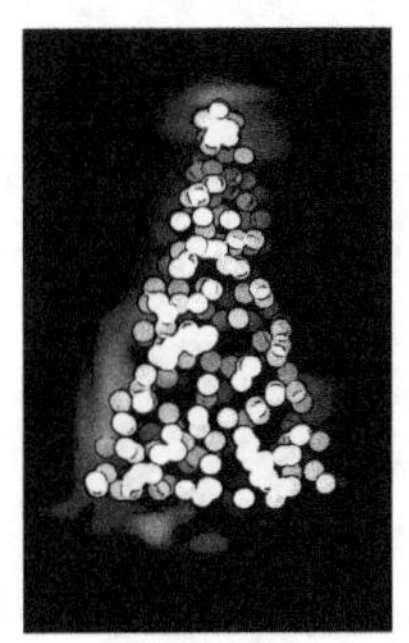

They didn't want to eat their doggies. Some must have cried, or wanted to–or were afraid to. They were never fed, so they were always hungry. Old men made them hunt their food or steal it. And if they caught a girl...

That's how you make boys wolves.

Beneath the metallic tree Streamly Gredible pressed herself into the couch with Marbles at her feet and Gracie flopping heavy across her chest. Stretching, she sweetly appreciated soft dogs so near while glumly imagining hard boys so far. A finger wriggled to tickle a twitching ear. A toe extended to rub a groaning gut.

Ages later, Romans crucified dogs who didn't bark at Gauls. But they never forced boys to butcher finger licking doggies to become blood faced fighting men: wolf packs. Wolf raised Romulus murdered his brother and led a pack to rape Sabine Women. Did they roast their Wolf Mom on the solstice to toothpick her bones on some dirty, lurid, torchlit floor?

She wondered what tribesmen of the plains did to girls to make them feel like women? Maybe nothing. Girl's bodies tell in such ungentle ways. And then they get babies: little boys grown to be wolved.

It was all for war.

Weak warriors meant butchered men and bitter slavery for the rest. In Obby's war, NAZI subs were wolf packs too. He'd been a slave, and she had touched him, pressed her face into his shirt, and held his hand on rainy walks. She'd seen his coffin scrape into too tight a grave, and wars still scorched everywhere. Just not on Dryad's Lane. Yet.

The NAZIs didn't kill her Obby, but they had their chance. And NAZIs never murdered her dud. Anti NAZIs killed him dead. But NAZIs didn't kill her mud. NAZIs didn't kill her mud. NAZIs didn't kill her mud.

***

It was afternoon. As the day was dimming quickly toward dusk, the Yuletide twinkling grew more discernible. Breakfast, snack, and lunch plates still littered the floor, but Carol would make her take supper at the table so it was time to move. The doggies needed to be outside and were letting her know.

At least once per day now, Gracie'd rasp and gasp wide-eyed for air. She had nearly as many years as Greta, and that was old for a dog.

Very old; poor Gracie!

Hairy white Marbles had her heavy doggy smell, but Gracie's sweet brown fur was like sniffing grape Kool-Aid. Greta pushed her nose in and breathed hot breaths.

Poor Gracie! Live forever, girl!

She squeezed tight the old baby doggie who struggled

back with sharp paws bruising tender breasts and then, still blanket wrapped, stumbled toward the kitchen's back door so both babes could dash out wagging.

She surveyed the fridge. Maybe she should cook? Blue Apron made everything a cinch. But so many pots and pans. So much standing up. So many ways to make a mistake. A burning house is a holocaust too.

Footscuffing, she ripped the bedclothes from the sofa, tossed them into her computer closet, and then racked her crusty dishes in the empty washer. She thumbed the paper slips, then shoved them under the drop cloth shielding the floor from imaginary needles never shed by fiberoptic Tannenbaums.

> December 9. 1980
> He was the closest to being anyone I knew. I saw him standing there in the dark at the edge of the crowd not holding a candle. He was trying not to cry before recognizing me doing the same and said hi. I guess we had to say something. "It's a drag, innit?" That meant Paul wasn't coming.
> We'd missed poor Ringo, but

the crowd had shielded him from itself. What if George came? Would he be OK? People need to protect each other from each other. So why were we there now? Why hadn't we been there then? Why hadn't somebody been there to stop him?

We walked away. Into the park and were werewolves together. We were vampires. Afraid of no evil, we sucked up the dark. We held hands. It was just a night thing. We howled, snapped, and pawed. Our teeth clashed. It was a night thing.

His name is Abe. Avram Ider.

I don't know who Ezra Pound is.
And just a tit about Jerry Lewis
Why do I hafta know?

I know who's Winston O Boogie,
Paul Ramone, and Dwarf MacDougle too
They mean bigly things to little me
Because they meant something too cool to you two.

I'm gonna know things that you'll never
You're not gonna shade my life forever
John Coltrane might be a deity
Just not in the Vatican or Salt Lake City.

Winds might spread me out like smoke
Floods might wash my dust away
The sun might bleach my hair and bones
What I knew alone might die with me today.

I don't know who voted for Hitler
I don't know who wants to kill me
I don't know the mud I came from
Or even if my dud was the fucking one.

I can hardly take a step
Or tell a soul what dreams run through me
We only say whatever's been said
We only read whatever's been read
We only hear whatever's been heard
We only see one sliver of thread.

I don't know where the hell you went
I don't know what the hell you meant
Why do I hafta know?
Merry Fucking Christmas and Happy Hairy Hanukkah

"That's good. What's wrong with that?"

"You helped me."

"You help me. People long dead before I ever breathed help me. You know that. That's what this is about. See? But what shall you call it?"

"I dunno."

"'Hafta'?"

"No."

"'Hafta Have a Merry Freaking Christmas'?"

"Are you kidding?"

"'Legacy'?"

"Fuck no."

"What does it make you think of?"

"Me mud and me dud found each other in Central Park."

"They met in a Philosophy class."

"No."

"No?"

"No. They didn't know each other's names until they met in the ducking dark that night."

"'Werewolves of Yesterday pre-Strawberry Fields, Central Park'?"

"Maybe... Nah."

"'Dakota Meme a Thing to Me'?"

"Stop it."

"So... 'Untitled by Greta Van Ider: Too Cool for School'?"

"Uh Uh. I already have enough untitleds."

"'I Don't Know What Never Means'?"

"'I Don't Know Where Never Minds'."

"That might be good. 'Never Mind Pappy. I'm Only Reading'?"

"Nope."

"That's Bob Dylan ya know."

"I don't, you know. Let's keep him outta this, please... But I don't know what never means. I don't know what never ends. I don't know what never mends. I don't know what heaven sends. I don't know what seven spends. I don't know eleven rends. I don't know

whatever... *What I don't know, I don't know alone. 'What I don't alone know, I'll never forget.' That's it."*

"Better write it down."

February 2, 1993

I never knew there was really such a thing as an electric violin, but I knew the boy playing it. At least I knew him once for one mad sad night when he was such a boy which he so obviously still is.

But this time I learned about his father. Rather I found whose son he was. I'd just seen his dad at the Bryant Library and that old man still haunts me still. Someone so sad. So spare. So alone. So frail. But the strength it took to survive what he withstood so young is beyond my capacity to even dream—despite whose daughter I am. Thinking these stories is like trying to set comfortably while a child screams full faced behind a screen of silence—as unreachable as any projection beyond touch or control.

And this Avram Ider! I wanted to smack or switch him off like static. I almost felt myself shoving the table into his gut and flipping it against his face so coffee mugs would smash and bitter brew would scald him. Once was enough, he said of his Abba's lectures, but couldn't admit this was his own frail timidity. He HAD to be insufferably dismissive in the most bullish, dickish, blowhardy way. I get enough haughty insouciance from my own hollowed sire.

But how could I not know we bled with the same wound? Who am I to despise someone unready to descend those deep depths even though in his father is a willing, strong, and gentle guide—unlike my grim provider.

And we're both motherless! It didn't even seem strange talking about children we should NEVER have. This is not biology. These are necessities so far beyond! And whatever he thinks he wants from me, I know I have a deeper sense of his deeper needs. And that I can, somehow, help us both understand.

She traipsed upstairs and, sockfoot, kicked open the door to her nominal bedroom. There she gathered pillows and cushions, some ransacked from extraneous rooms, to fashion herself a nest on the bed's empty flatness where she uncomfortably curled with Marbles and Gracie squirming in.

Writhing and breathing dog breaths, she tried leering down the ceiling or glaring out windows at tree shrieked skies, but the mantel boxes had summoned to garrote her attention. With spare darkness they stared back in a stern concert never orchestrated when their bone crumbs bore flesh.

Their fathers, still full formed, lay buried where Well-Wood shomers kept their watch, but weren't these here, their springoffs, at her mercy?

They could be mixed with cement and molded into gargoyle figurines. Dud could be sculpted into a horny chubby Kokopelli chasing corny coeds with humpfulls of trinkets and furs. Mudd's ashes could form a hissing dryad, rootbound but arching up to slash back with razor twigged branches.

Then she thought *"felt feet"*. Their boxy sarcophagi needed green scratchproof pads glued beneath. She grabbed the caskets and set them on a checker-work of books arrayed over bedcovers, sliding them like fat kings and queens up, down, over, and around, sometimes clicking in gentle collisions. Enthralled to her, they glided from light to dark, red to green, black to tan, hardcover to paperback with butt shaking, Lindy Hopping, and just a bit of doggy style humping.

P and M.
P and M.

All is calm.
 I'm with them.

Sound young virgin so slender and wild
I'm not pregnant cuz I'm still undefiled
Sleep in heavenly pieces . . .
Sleep in dead ember peace.

She lifted the two boxes above her head in solemn blessing.

Ashes from smashes and dust to gusts. . .

Should she open a window and pour them out?

Have Yourself some Sooty Little Cinders . . .

Maybe they'd leave a streak across the snow that would last till the spring and then stain the roof?

O Ashes We Have Calcified. . .

Maybe together they could scuttle out and simply perch in the cold wet wind until someone looked up above the porch to seem them crouched?

I'll Have a Flu Chimney Without You . . .

"Jump! Jump! Jump!" rude wassailers would chant

until pelted with parental ashes choking their throats and stuffing their noses.

O There's no Place for Bones for the Holidays
...In Excelsis Gloria...

December 11, 2003

It's official.

I know it makes no sense to be angry at Abe, but I am, I can't help it, and so why hide it? It wasn't his idea, but what is, and anyway he's complicit as all hell. I'm livid at myself too. And I'm angry at this bitter little bloodsucking homunculus of a cell cluster.

I can't help thinking it's a girl, and that is so infuriating!

I don't want any baby. But to not breed is to submit to their deathful victory. Abba Ider was so sweet when he learned the news. "You must be strong. You know I'll help you." And the way he arched his eyebrow toward that lump of his son! We shared a smile.

My own chuff chuffing black shoe Daddy just grinned, but not even at me. He just chuffed me off and grinned at Abey. It wasn't even a grin though. It was a leer. "Now vut?" And he laughed his silent, breathless laugh.

But if I am to give life, I want it to be a

> boy. Why? I know girls are stronger—or thought I did. Would I worry less about a boy? Would I identify less?
>
> Oh, please let it not be a girl.

Streamly Gredible, leaving her rumpled bed all book-strewn, replaced her parents on the mantel shelf. She padded downstairs to her sleeping place sofa and tried to cuddle herself into slumber.

"Maybe someday I'll have nothing to prove."

Forty-One

Mother Love

In which, under the inspiration of J. Winston Legthigh's Dublinesque precursor, the most rotund progenitor of Greddly Mayfilly Aidler all sprawlingly propounds upon some maternal concatenations, the perils of personhood, the meaningful meanings of meanings, power, and certain other uncertain spivactory bases of modern unrefined Chelonialism.

Greetings my diminutive chickadee, my heavenly little wren, and "Yellow

Chickenbutt Stranger Danger on irascible rollerblades"!

That's you, Gredible![1]

So how are you today? And, nearly almost as unimportant, how are I?[2]

No matter what, I love you hopelessly godawfully much and so does your vacuum-sealed ashpacked mother. Now please note how I write of the Mud in the presentable tense even although you're personally still (as I type this) long hauling her steelrolled cremains all round the Northeast in your dreary little knap-

---

[1]   *Are you at all adenoid at being called all these names"? It's just my contretemps to mature you it's really me scrawling this to you - and only to you. No one else! And it's eating away at me that this is even a concern, but there's a certain way to my dismay I'm sure to fade someday from your memory with my borrowed voice only a scratchy fleshless echo full of flimflam and pretense. And yes, we are also inseparable parts of one another, but we're unavoidably a part of everything else just as all the rest is imparted in us, but there are times when I only* want to think of you while simperingly wishing you save a special spot in your meme scheme for me, your fat old dummy daddy.

[2]   *Am I in the next room, another town, or "in another 'state'"? Logic tells me if you're reading this, you're somewhat extant and, hopefully, well; . . . the reciprocal is obviously less than guaranteed. But if I'm available to you (as in only a knock, a holler, a phone call, text, email, or some other new-fangled mode of annoyance - other than the Ouija Board - away), I pray you will try to conjure me before scrolling much further.*

sack. But by NOW I might be smashed ashes as well.[3]

And before THIS is finished, I'll probably get rounded to tissuing some fartherly[4] advice. In the meantime, I must return to infirming what's already been amplified: which is that my love for you should endure wrong after I'm mantel-pieced in some tastefully encasing urn[5].

I'm really groan to try to put some steel behind the ideal my love for you will survive my hard-faltering heartbeats but must first remind you to steadfastly ignore any shimmer of obligation you might EVER feel to peruse this in any

---

[3] Somewhere along the line (maybe it's on my driver's license) I may have authorized the donation of some portions of me (maybe the eyes?) or other. If I get around to it, I really should volunteer more organs (if they're actually good for anything) to the deservedly needy though I'm decidedly strangely still bothered by the idea of becoming a practice cadaver for some apprentice quack, but perhaps I should try to get over such stiflings be forrest too late.

[4] call me "Paternal Polonius"!

[5] *While we're on the subject if in the end, you do go with "tasteful", could it be a vessel that's relatively tall and slender? Slender is, after all, a lifelong ambition . . . then again, I'm not against anything that makes you smile - even if it means some period of knapsack purgatory . . . And don't get all bulimic on me because of some moronic "slim" comment just now laden onto my already heaping pile of legacy moronia you may never be able to fully "emerge" from!*

steadfast way. It's spuriously not necessary[6].

I supposedly respect you probably will (eventually) continue to spread this through to the witless end. So, I also need to discourage any nexpectation such reading might be nespecially worthwhile[7]

The first disorder of business is to affirm my love for you continues neverlending and will extend despite me, despise my state of being or non-being, despirit how I've hurt you, disparage how I failed you, and despecially how much I continue to burden you[8]. The same goes for your mother, and yes, I do dare to squeak for her[9].

Now it is, as they say in BeanTown, "not a

---

[6] *Not now. Not ever. By the way . . . is there really anything I can say to you that would really be helpful now? I mean this as an open, non-argumentative question. I mean this as something to consider before you read any further, as you continue to read, and well after you've finished reading.*

[7] *Well, actually I'm worried whatever I write might actually be the OPPOSITE even if (perhaps nespecially if) my words are understood as I intend them to be: a ludicrous aspiration in so many ways. But someone (was it E. B. White?) once wroted that writing is an "act of faith" - as if that would differentiate it from anything else a human can do. But "faith" is such a loaded and compromised concept . . . Anyway, that's how it is to me. (Been "saved" yet?)*

[8] You don't have to put all my charred bones in your baggie. Just a little pinch could serve jest as swell to assuage your scoliosis.

[9] In fact, it's a main purpose of my writing here.

shocka" to affirm your Mud was not a good mother in any conventional way. There's a mound of probable evidence you knew this was how it would always be well before I belatedly so discerned and well before you could speak more than a squawk. And Herself, almost immediately postpartum, swore she could see it in your accusingly affronted infant eyes[10].

I know as I write this, not only that may I not tell you anything really new or helpful; I might not even tell you anything sparticularly convincing. For one thing, either you're arterially conveined of my love for you—or you're not. I'm afraid you might already be convicted your mother did not. But she DID love you strainfully much whether or no any singsong could ever assure you of that. And despite all else, she was your mother. And she was good.

Yes. She. Was.

(Is!)

10
   And (though I managed to keep it to myself) the same thought passed questionably through my own distracted mind more than once. But we never really know what we see. And hope clings maternal.

Now, of course, she did not love you in the way she would liked to, the way we all think others expected her to, in the way (perhaps) you would have wanted, in ANY way ANY infant is primed to expect—or anything near what we're told they REQUIRE from some reasonable surrogate[11]. But love you she did, and BOY, did she love you, girl!

Unfortunately, your mother, let's be frank, did not necessarily love you as a person[12].

This is where it gets so difficult and is perhaps one reason why I shrink to talk down to you about your mother. Or anyway it's an excuse I might rely upon wrong after I can't use the tenderness of your rage as a resort. It may partly be

[11] By the way, I know I was an UNREASONABLE surrogate, but more than one helpful shrink (I'd like you to know) said I was "good enough" and if you're reading this or (capable of) doing so in some relatively non-medicated unfrantic state, then maybe I was?

[12] In fact, you're much more than any "PERSON" as if that were anything to brag about. At some point it's likely you have felt (or will feel) urgently compelled to believe the most important thing you could do was to experience yourself (and be experienced) as a person, but whatever you do (or have done) in some crummy dorm room with other consenting morons should forever remain your own dirty business as far as I'm concerned. But more pertinently there are so many yous in you and so many of hers in her loud loving loose corridors of possibilities that your yous manifest. Und, I'm knot even gretting into loik v luv.

the zeitgeist of your generation, but it's also our deplorable parenting that makes you now such a mistress of "Shock and Are" employed, perhaps, to preempt familial disclosures and confidences which more straight-faced parents consider so inappropriate. But whatever compels them, such measures on your part have a regrettable tendency to convey an exaggerated impression of a sophistication and mature capacity to cope with jarring speculations, divulgences, or revelations regarding the parent-child bond as well as innumerable other contingencies of human interactions whether they be intimate, cultural, historical, or theoretical. On this front, I will always regret I was not MUCH more intentional about fostering your fortitude instead of possibly undermining it, and I pray to the Turtlehead my sense of your resilience is not too over-exaggerated.

I don't know why I berated so long around the brush for this. Maybe I should have spit it right out on top of this here epistle in an upper title case? (The "not a shock value", if any, might make you chuckle[13].)

---

[13] But what if it somehow joltz? (Guess it deep ends on the stage that plays you at the thyme of this reeding)

And since we're being frank, I feel the need to reemphasize how I always feel the pinch of scrinching eggshells beneath my stained sock feet whenever I even think about conversing with you about Herself, your mom, no matter how resilient you prove yourself to be over and over and over again and again.

Persons or personalities do crack up. It occurs to me it actually happens to everyone if they're lucky and, at that, more than once. Sometimes it's dramatically abrupt. Or it can be more like a slow protean flow. As I write this, I'm aware I've never sat you down and mansplained how your poor, ever-frenzied, Mommy took her own life. Maybe I'm writing this now because I'm afraid I'll never get to it while I still heave with my own weakening lungs? Of course, there's some chance you'll stumble cross this before I shimmy off my mortal coils, which would give you the nopportunity to decide whether and how to emotionally eviscerate me for my cowardly insensitivity? Go on! I can take it![14]

Have you yet given much thought to the

[14] (Maybe.)

differences between what are called "persons" and "personalities"? Do you think they're like layers? Certainly, a "personality" has different parts, with some uncertain quirks, preferences, predilections, and temperaments more long-lasting than others. Do you think a "personality" can reasonably be compared to a set of clothes: some basic hygienic undies–or, perhaps, the frilly or provocative kind tucked below various (more or less) practical or stylistic layers and accoutrements[15]? Can a "person" ever be "naked" in the sense of "stripped of all personality"? But even if "personality" is not separable from "personhood" aren't there some parts that are more variable, and even more exchangeable, than others[16]?

---

[15] Of course, it could be a glow! And of course, it is more than like an energetic radiation than it is like any garment or even a skin which when rudely rent or roughly abraded is selfully reconstituted by definitional cellular directions sent from ancestral DNA.

Nut, then again, a glow is a particulate wavering emanation from sub-elementary interactions, but all we godawful gods and goddesses are clothed in light even when bashfully starkers.

[16] I'm sure you don't think a person is the same as its personality? Or maybe you do. Do you? Am I confusing? Am I confused? Either way, how many elements of a personality could be chopped away before there is another (or no) person?

What about the terms "self" and "identity"? Do any such ideas disturb you sufficiently to think of them for more than an irritated instance? Maybe you've surpassed that "stage" of development where such preoccupations have any special moment? I, "personally" think it's impossible to ponder "identity" without confronting the "multiple mirrors" by which we almost cannot help but see ourselves through the (often imaginary) eyes of "others." But I also think this absurdity is part of our humanity: one of our defining contraventions.

Your mother, like the patriarchal cultures of capitalism, racism, domination, and Studio-Christianity is part of you, and you are part of me in ways that go far beyond shared genetics. Don't ever forget Uncle Stan and Aunt Carol were a part of your life (a piece of you) due (in very large particle) from so early on because of your Mum. And don't underestimate how much this was a torturous, semi-public galling self-rebuke she grimly endured as a sacrifice toward your wellbeing – or toward the potentialities for any such a notion.

 It was never the fact of your birth – or

your existence – that crushed in upon her. NEVER!

Reproach her for not being another person. Reproach her for abandoning you. Reproach her for not leaving you sooner. But if you have any mercy or tenderness at all, do NOT imagine she ever willed anything but "good" for you...at least not since you bravely gulped your first gasps of breathable air. Never imagine she EVER put her "comfort" (what a joke!) or well-being ahead of yours. That would be SUCH a very agonizing injustice[17].

I know from the troubles of my own childhood and adolescence the best way to hurt your parents is to hurt yourself. I know from loving your mother that much of what she did to hurt herself was to somehow hurt her own P&M—and not just your lonely old Zeyde, but her own soul-absconding mother. This shared pain (and shared joy) is a painful truth about pain and truth and love and humans that might be too simple for any of us to understand?

---

[17] But that children don't owe their parents justice is me nimble nopinion!

And I swear upon a stack of turtles your mother never inflicted any injury upon herself to EVER reproach or damage YOU!!! It was always sooo much the opposite, and the idea you might not understand or believe this stabs me now in ways that must also hurt you—and your sky shattered Mudd[18].

In his retirement, my own dad, your Abba/ Obby became enchanted with crafting pitiful little stories. And I know he was never satisfied with those he wove. They were, he was only too hellishly aware, awkward attempts to help himself crumb to terms with old ordeals endured during the formative atrocities of his epigenetic[19] development during the goodest war of the EGreedious Degeneration. It was a bigger part of his melancholy that each attempt only seemed to spread him ever farther from what he pined for so lucidly, so earnestly, and so hopelessly. He was inwardly urged to somehow help people scope with a world so liable to generating the tripe of wrenching treacheries such as

---

[18] Have I ever, before you read this, tried to explain this eye to eyeful? You don't need to forgive me if I haven't. But have I here put this in words that could possibly explain anything?

[19] ...try, Try, TRY! to eat good food and think good thoughts - if only for your innocent born great-grandchildren - if you should ever happen to spill any.

befell him and his (your) decimated family. But such is a worthy calling to any soulful elder. And, of course, it's the agony of every parent who doesn't shrink from their ultimate, intimate, incremental responsibility.

In the Beginning

There might have been an egg.
Filled with universes of potential
It lay stiff-shelled and cocooned
Warmed under the fetid haunches of its bird
progenitors.

Inside itself, it churned and swirled
Until one day it beaked through
Some flimsy windings and then OUT its brittle
box.

Soon, blind and soaking,
It gaped open its maw:
A command no parent could fail to but obey.
And the egg, outside its firstly shell,
Now ruled imperiously a smaller much realm
Only composed of nest and the cold open sky
Still waiting thunderously above.

Eventually, came the day when the egg felt its
most tiny and alone
As it dived from the nest to catch wind beneath
awkward wings,
So it could swoop above wispy clouds,
Plummet toward sparking water,
Or skim rapidly the fringe tips of reaching
trees,
The swirls of restless rivers,
And the snowy rocked tops of lonely mountains.

But then, mostly,
It was blissfully at one
With the skins
Of sky and snow and water and trees
Which, tangled together by light,
Formed an intermingling barrier under the shell
of the sky
That cracked closed closer only on rare black
nights
When there was no moon to gleam
From the colliding eyes of turtles***

*You my love are, at least partially, an
emergency. Like space and time and
everything we know, you are an
emergency capable of overwhelming
anyone unprepared – and there will be*

circumstances when you are among that uncertain "some."

You, my love, are an emergency and a generator of new emergencies!

But you are also so much more than that.

Emergency and the ever-emerging emergence of countless new realities is how I (don't[20]) make sense of "everything".

Emergencies like "consciousness" or "wetness" can never be fully explained or understood by their substrates or by their component parts which themselves are only "prior" para-emergencies with their own non-determinant components. And, as science must inevitably agree, no ever-changing layer of component-based "reality" is ever fundamental. The only "fundamental"[21] might (not) be emergence itself which represents (or rather not is) an unbounded dynamo of oneness.

[20] And can't! But the only tools now available to my decimating mind are the WORDS I can affix to this virtual paper! But as for "emergencies" . . . well "emerging" might be a fundamental (I hate THAT word) aspect of the multiverse, but that doesn't mean it's THE fundamental aspect. And even truly NEW "emergent realities" have aspects that may be "timeless".

[21] Why must there be anything fundamental or ultimate? We are a strange loop of loops.

Nothing emerges that wasn't already.

> *We don't know what we're talking about. Not even close. Especially when we talk about "reality". We talk about "reality" whenever we stink we should be taken seriously. We are being "grave", but the word "gravity" has been perverted by the Newtonians as well as by Einsteinians who see it as a warping of space-time which they tell us (I'm sure correctly) can involve contractions, expansions, twists, and even rends.*

But, whenever[22] I consider myself; I am only a limited pinprick inhibited by my gravely semiconscious orientation in time and space. Therefore, despite all objections, I sometimes feel the repellent requirement for some empirically doomed "sense" of "foundation".

Leaving aside the question of "dimensions," can I propose that the only important directions in space are outward and inward? Would you consider this? The first, driven by what might be called either "inflationary expansion" or "entropy[23]" might be the more

---

[22] I thought I was wavering until I pricked myself and found I was particulate.

[23] or whatever supersedes such a vague and contradictory concept - and which relates (perhaps in some loopy way) to acceleration.

powerful[24]. *The second, (the inward direction/pull) is also matholinguistically susceptible to acceleration. It might mistakenly be called "gravity"–and not just because of an understandable (but misleading) propensity that might mislead us to compare it with "falling.[25]" But gravity must be something all together else! This inward falling into the bottomless infinitesimal may well be just another form of graceful entropy.*

Time, more emphatically, appears to be additionally constrained in terms of having only two directions–in that we tend not to imagine any axes other than forward and back, but with the each of those accessible to us only in certain sperms of our imagination[26].

---

[24]*Note how Chelonialism **merely** APPEARS to comport with current conventions in physics which insist on conflating forces with geometry?*

Now you, at your slender age, are already more well versed in Mathematics than I ever were, but doesn't Calculus equate force with slope? Or maybe I'm just muddled once again? But it really doesn't matter because I reject all Math and Geometry - or at least any assertions they are less deceptive than the rest of our senselessness.

[26] *And, still, somehow, we're expected by some to keep in mime the idea that "time" is an inseparable aspect of whatever subsumes it with the rest of "space". But that's only one of the most problematic conundrums of the "whatever" we intuit to be "time." (As Mr. Harrison so plaintively complained, "It's All Too Much!")*

Flying out and falling inward might be better metaphors for the "dimensions" of space[27] than are our conventions of Cartesian gridlock, but they're probably no less metaphorically inept—and maybe not even too much more (or less) metaphorical. And anyway, the metaphors inside our minds (not brains[28]?) cannot be totally derided justly because they are <u>only</u> mental constructions. Pale Platonic reflections they may be, but they do enable some "level" of survival. So why totally reject other hints into the unseen we may intuitively experience conceptually, bodily, or emotionally such as those conveyed via art, music, or passion itself?

Imagination clearly resembles a form of creative emergence. What of it if it has no apparent tangible manifestation[29]? Based on the best of our empirically and logically confirmed knowledge of nature (physics), we have ever less ration to doubt the existence of "dimensions" that

---

[27] Dimensions are themselves a contingent and questionable catalog of concepts.

[28] "Net brains"?

[29] But isn't imagination constantly generating new (sometimes) tangible spamifications, ain't they? (Always resemble who best pled us never to forget to "IMAGINE"!

may (or may not) exist both within and beyond our fatally limited frame of reference which the pocket protector set so lamely considers "geometrical."

Imagination and morality (perhaps extending far beyond what we measure as mercy, justice, or reciprocity) may well be our beast indications of dimensions (or inwoven levels of reality) that actually give partial emergence to the limpid space and invisible time which seems to underpin all our grievous whinings.

My darling, it's becoming uncomfortably (obscenely?) obvious to me, that I'm increasingly falling under the grip of some unspeakable urge to convince you to see well beyond any comical image of Yurtles stacked precariously on piles of subreluctant terrapins when considering Chelonialism[30]. Yes, this is my most serious amusement, but it may well be neither amusing nor serious to you. Go forth and create by your own enticing lights[31].

---

[30] *which neither can be reliably conveyed via the lamentable metaphor of infinitely self-encased Russian Turtle Dolls*

[31] **said Polonius to Ophelia under the shifting shadows of terrapin myst formations**

<u>*But dredging upward, corporeal tangibility is unceasingly overrated. There is so much "concrete" (or metallic) "reality" that can be overturned, rent, exploded, or pulverized much more readily than any tinpot lout can demolish a social convention or abolish an institution.*</u> *And this suggests another metaphor (aside from encasement or stackability) for how realities or dimensions can pervade each other as part of a perpetual reshaping and twisting that defies any staid set of geometric conceptions or equations.*

I think of Jimmy Joyce in the guise of Schlepping Deadliest sludging through an imaginary Schlublin, and as we were told, temporarily assuming (or being possessed by) various subcultural roles and antisocial categories. First, he is a son. Then father or brother. At the same time, he may be a suitor or a poet, a debtor or a joker, a murderer or thief, an ad canvasser or a masturbator, a librarian, or an inseminally malpracticing med student. The ghosts of Hamlet, Spamlet's ghostly father and ghastly algebraic grandfather may pass through his essence, taking for a tempo full hold of his slimagination and indemnity. Then he is Simon Daedalus or Father Long John Slipperinner before he

*becrumbs Icarus or Iago or Oscar Wilde,
Saul McCarsky (Matron Molly Came to Be),
or Algernon Rodentwhiskers – or elks they
beslum him. You, my precious little
imperious maiden, may yet become a
mother and then a crone but, Turtles or
no, there are so many other ulterior
dimensions to churn, fulfill, possess,
define, taunt, delight, and torture you.*

Regret

The weight and push of history is
Also the pull of the future.
And there is no direction there.
No up. No down.
Maybe no in or out.
Trying to hold on.
Trying to let go.
A better world.
Protection and Preparation.
Binaries, mosaics, whirligigs,
Quantum states
Nothing is fundamental.
We are condemned to
(not)
Wallow in dichotomies
Relating to courage and compassion,
Autonomy nor dependence,
Or even gravity and grace.

Inward or outward are equally generative. Equally creative. There is no bottom, no top, no inner core or outer limit. And even within each pulminating imaginary onion ring, there is churning and changing and shifting and switching that constantly generates new combinations that add incremental submergencies onto differing "ultradimensional" axes. For instance… in the realm of human social-emotional mimetic and tonsorial cultures…there's imagination and hope, music and yearning…

Maybe I don't believe any person has some true inner "core." Maybe it's just my own pathology, cowardice, or stupidity treacherously prompting me to "honestly" claim I never found one in me. To me 'personal essence' is something akin to the idea of "Yankee" which to the blessedly benighted rest of the world is any natural born (maybe white…) citizen of the US[32].

If you think of 'meaning' or 'significance'

---

[32] But to we 'Muricans, a "Yankee" is merely someone born north of the Mason-Dixon Line. But within that realm, the term can only apply to New Englanders, any of whom would summarily direct an inquisitor toward the hills of Vermont among whose denizens are suspender-wielding retired dairy farmers who miserly ladle maple syrup over their a la moded apple pie for Sunday special breakfasts.

only as alternate ways of repeating something using different words, there may be no meaningful meanings no matter how many may scream to be (more or less) interesting. But meanings MUST transcend words. And if you can accept that language is no more "meaningful" than any other creative process, while avoiding the idea of any "ultimate" meaning, then you can entertain the idea that "meaning" could be ever-increasing (in its own "unitary" way, of course[33]).

Now a political ninterlude:

Meaning equates to power which is politics which is the myth[34] of human significance. I'm not preaching to you about ideologies. But those who hold power illegitimately (meaning they don't use it to benefit the human community) do everything they can to disparage and diminish meaning just as they do

---

[33] But what does any of this have to do with the price of Molly Malone? (Think about it, please!) Doesn't meaning's "meaning" merge into less idealistic ideas of "value"? – or "**power**"!

[34] There's still more moment in myth than in the craftiest equations or the most deeply chiseled laws and histories. But we're corn prone to either idiotically rely on more paltry forms of terrorizing intimidations or else on crafting numbing mirages of inevitability and lack of alternative with witch to enmesh our victims. (Someday I might sort this out, but the empty wind could also be left to you to out-untangle any bits that might bear the scrutiny of lantern-eyed Lucifer.)

everything possible to divide the human community when they are not assiduously denying its existence. Gravity might not be the fall into the blessed white rabbity hole where space slips out of time into quantum plunges ever plummeting. It might be what holds us steadily transfixed between infinite inflation and neverlasting precipices of phantom inwardness. But without the widening uplifting gyre of entropic "grace" what's left might be the unredeemable stasis of sinful self-entrenchment.

Each of us has an inborn individual propensity to abuse and dominate others. It's something that transcends mere selfishness because we are all liable to "feel" ourselves exalted by the degradation of others. Call it "sin." Or go even deeper into our "nature" (physics) and call it gravity. It's not all evil and maybe somewhat relationally about defining things (including our "selves" as "separate") and wanting them to cohere[35].

But just as powerful (probably MUCH more...?) is what blends us, spreads us

---

35 And, of course, persist

out, and "uplifts" us beyond ourselves. Call it "grace" or call it "entropy." (It's even more exhilarating because it dissolves all boundaries – annihilating even those that define our "selves")

This all gets complexified by our perplexity to agglomerate in groups and klaverns and compounds and polymers of tribal nonsense necessary for sour bible. But such dynamite[36] remains chain reactive at all levels of inadvisability.

Aside from the inevitably compelling, but not fully reliable, indications of our corporeal emotions we understand "meanings" as examples of "reference." But this still "means" EVERY form of creativity is "meaningful", more or less since they always, at least, refer back to their creator. And yes, this view of "meaning" allows one to argue some

---

[36] Energy and power are imbalances as much as relationships. We "detect" them as intermittent particles which don't exist even though certain types of "measurements" might tell someone where something pointlike might once have been destroyed or absorbed even though our second-best logic and evidence tell us it had no "real" prior existence.

Imbalances, irregularities, disturbances, and emergencies are all other words for matter and energy.

As if words themselves created categories. (Do they have that power? Whaddya think?)

creations may be more meaningful[37] than others if only based on our limited capacities to quantify any additional creations such may generate or inspire. It might be equally "valid" to (backwardswise) count the number of creators and inspirations involved in the generation of any "particular" creation. If this line of thought should happen to bring to mind any idea of ex nihilo virginal burps, then I'm happy you've even got this far no matter how nonsensical and or pretentious you find this (me) to be. But if we're into designing scoring systems[38], I'm enthusiastically in favor of granting super originality points for anything that even APPEARS to pop outta some void. And no, I won't here try to define or redefine "nothingness" or argue anything about its "existence" in or out of the "here and now".

---

[37] Meaning "powerful"!

[38] The Night Before Larry Got Stretched he Kurzweiled his penultimate PageRank.

Space and Time

To define is to have power over.
To define is to limit
***Gravity* is Scylla definition**
***Grace* is Charybdis escape**
Do you really wanna find yourself?
Do you really wanna know who you are?
Are you really that serious?
You are not just a rope
You are not just a bridge
You are not just a stepping stone.
You are everything.
Perpetually creating itself
You are everything.

Rounding back to YOU...

Popping out a child is one possible result of a certain type of pair bond – though such may, by the time you read this, not even be physically necessary for the emergency in question[39]. As for your

[39] But creativity must also involve the preservation of older configurations so I'll ignore this likelihood for now.

*mother and eye, we were first dreamers,
our minds filled with ink-squirting squids
and myst-bellowing wizards*[40]*. Early on
we learned the futility of explaining
ourselves to each mother.*

*Only later did we fail to generate enough
delight between us.*

*Squeaking of language, your vestal
mummer unimmaculate distrusted,
more than anything, the glib*[41] *whom, in
the juices of youth, she'd sally forth with a
very odd earnestness to mock and counter
and confound at every importunity. But
that's not just because shit talkers rarely
have anything to say or to offer—it's that
they so often tend to get the last word in
ways that stultify or obscure the kinds of*

[40] • *. . .in the stylistic confines of punk rock nihilism Mull of Kintyre.*

[41] Unfortunately, for all us squawkers, talk is nigh impossible to avoid. The self-generating web of language is also a drag that grabs us back gravitationally more than, as a scaffold, it props us up precariously to perceive new possibilities (before one of its crafty trapdoors springs up under our fluttering feets.)

Since (obviously?) spacetime is not the ground beneath our being, there's more to language than greets the I. Like logic and maths, it has ghastly tendrils into and outfrom what we quaintly think of as "our" thinking or "our" minds (also dually distinct but intermingled entities.*) Still pointy heads do what they can to coin new words to evershed the murk of commonplace connotations. Perhaps I should try the same since the intermingled concepts of "dimension" v "universe" v "reality" are already so venereally enmeshed.

*meaning that ennoble human struggle[42].
Tragic insouciance! That's how your
callow reject P&M staggered together,
somehow managing to keep our grades
up. But that in its initial most puerile
form was not what crafted you who were
belatedly inseminated only after the bulk
of unpent youthful spunk was sapped by
the deflating arrows of time—and even
then only after more than a dozen months
of acrimonious urgencies from one who
would not be denied or mocked out of*

Maybe some mighty mathematicians are not so totally enamoured of Rene's Coordinate Cartography because their enlightened equations need no coaxial graph paper. And maybe some other super perceptive stumblers recognize not only can grids be stacked alike Star Trek 3D Breast Boards (child's play for you, my hawklike girl?), but such tissues of realities can twist and funnel into and out of each other like molten paraffin in a lava lamp while multiple origins slip and glide from plane to waving plane when not blinking in and blotting out in their own parthenogenetic way.

So through the everloving mess of everything swing mind, language, consciousness, and spacetime. They smush into us as we share parts with them and many things (that are not things) outside our fields of dream. But I will wrestle with the words I've been groused with knowing grace may not be entropy and gravity too **night** be many more relationships than just the pulls of twisting time.

[*] *which is why everyone should learn Maths to make their trickster obscurities banal enough to push pointy heads farther forward.*

[42] **"God save the good samaritan and god save the Worthless Creep"**

joint by lamely conceived dismissals of biological cliched clocks because no such timekeeper ever tolled for you any more than you were effectually compelled by any jejunely affected vainglorious defiance of long dead murderous NAZI clerks or the banal heavy wraths that survive them still! ...And now, a musical ninterlude:

WondrunTown

by Saul Nigarsky (*fenzy zinger boy*)

Effrey two-bit McMurphy with his loving big fat nurse
Sits home watchn' TV for the better or for worse
Will tonight they bellow for an ambulance or simply call
a hearse?

Well, I don't know.

Thumb up. Drug down. I just don't know.

I DON'T KNOW. LET IT GO.

Acting like a jerk the S-Hole enervates his wife
With the same old ad-libs about entropy and light
Maybe he asphyxiates her with a butter knife?

We'll let it flow.

Downtown. Upside. Let it go.

I DON'T KNOW. I DON'T KNOW

Let's be real though—or at least as

toothful as possible. From my point of view, your conception and birth were actually major liberatory facets to my broke axle life, a development your mums could never overgag. I remember telling her skinny ass, not so long before she tripped away, how despite the dreamhaze of the Big RedEnd Chief, McMurphy deeply revered and abjectly depended upon HIS oversized Nurse. Now in my blind there might have been times your sainted mater, in her prematernal Artemis guise, would have been dairy delighted by this cruddy conceit, but by that pint matters were far too gunned down.

And, spin again, remember Actaeon.

Of course, those dogs still hurt and may yet rend me to bloody stripes though how or whether they tacked back upon the Lung Eyeland born avatar of their haunted goddess I know not. And now, how my body aches, and torpor lays everlurking for whenever I flail to outrun its mist in the early mud morning hours. But as the hemlock of decrepitude seeps inward from my extremities, I'm held buoyed just above the turgid wash in ways never experienced in my mistooken youth spent *submerged, holding only my breadth. Now seemingly nothing suffices to hold me down, though I know one day I'm damned to fail, boobing upward, salt faced to the spiny sun.*

But Louise Fletchered or not, your mum was[43] a caretaker, a guardian, a generous dispenser of boons. And I, partially intoxicated by my deliverance, could not communicate how much I needed her and earnestly pursued whatever ways what might appease her angry yearnings always gaping more urgently even as she threw up razor-wired blocks and posted resentful death breaching dragons to scorch every approach.

No matter how much we gnostically brought you upon our saddened selfs, lemme just say your emergence, first as a queasy foreboding, then as a shadowy sonogram, soon as a bumpy baby lump, a hard-kicking encumbrance, and then a caul shredding shrieker covered in blood and birthslime, was ultimately a gut slumping shock to us together both. Of course, that's eventually true of any

---

[43] primly and primarily

initial nativity to any gropesome couple no matter how unprepared, overconfident, set in their ways, unstable, youngered or eldred, or whatevered other form of clueless they were scoured to be.

Haven't I yet telled you how the many monthed preliminaries before your congestion featured (superficially at least) an ever-swelling maternal surge-up, which I[44] did my berry damnedest to turn off, skirt, trivialize, evade, derail, suppress, ignore, distract from, or squelch until, exhausted by effort and shamed by reproofs, I limply agreed to concede. But startling with the very first manifestations of your incipient existence, the roles of dread v wistful anticipation were reversed the way warmed waters in stratified spring-fed ponds can suddenly be overturned. The only distant constant was the downflow of your sainted mater's (extraneous) unsanctified tears. But this had never a hint to do with you as a person with any human agency.

Am I braying too much? Have I wheeled off the rails? Whatever else, lies and secrets

[44] (by Zeus! Not Hera!)

are also protections. But they're never merely "safe" guards: so liable they are to snap like booby traps indiscriminate as buried landmines aimed to maim long-forgotten enemies in erased populations extinguished ages ago by orchestrations of genocide. And this is why, when it comes to needy secrets, all I can guarantee is that I THINK I shouldn't really WANT to keep ANY from you, hoping against hope the powerfully protective offense of your own laughter can't or won't be turned against your own aching vulnerabilities[45].

Your ever-loving mummer's relationship to laughter is just one of those whats I never did got at. For her, for all I fail and failed to know, it was never a respected protection, certain forms of "safety" being among the stuffs she hotly and so scoldly always disdained. I cannot say either way, but maybe it was just because, whether sword or shield, there is a sort of laughter blackly furnaced by pain that evoked in her only horror and offense. And swords, forged of steel or crystalcut from hurt, can twist backways into taut unwary

[45] And of course, an egg can be an egg without its shell, but no matter how transversable or imaginarily blurry we seem to be defined by our protective definitions.

flesh or stab straight toward softly waiting wounds. Be so careful, Love.

Amongst us, some secrets were never stored away as such. They shrimply remained unspoken because their weight or energy[46] overcame the wrathful worth of words. Grant me some consideration here if you should someday trip across (or into) some scream left altogether undisclosed.

The way we self-protect can cripple us more than the scourging wounds of the "outside" they fight to fender off. And exertions to protect each other can spit out frightening lightning bolts that sparkle in our glim eyes the darkest weighty chains we forge to restrain the world's hurts as swell as our own instinctual uprisings we find better left pressed down under mountable layers of foundational sediments.

My long-doddering father, left to his own devisings would chuckle down the decency defying ant tricks of my childhood that sent my neurasthenic mother shimmying up spindly trees of unforced dramatic anguish. Lemme slake a mint to remonstrate me own darling departed

---

[46] or "mass" or "moment"

mutterer whom you never had the priv. "Oh!" she would deep snarl and high hiss into my blank face, frightened as she was at my future freight. "If you can't control yourself, the police and the penitentiary guards can an swill!" which frightened me not a bit. But one day the dolorous driving weight of her defeated desperate tearful sobs punctured my intransigence, injecting me with a heavy sense of consequence and hesitation.

But back to me dad and your own Obby. The later stages of my youth, however, prompted me to discern in his evershaky reserve a wounded delicacy that so enamored he to your sow, inducing her toward raptures of excessive solicitudes which he enjoyed with his customary mildly dyspeptic bemusement. This was something about your mum I never failed to find endearing, and feel spritely entitled to remark that you've understood this quite well too, for I've observed our old ladies' man evoke the same response from you. And smoldering umbrage is what I still tend to snake at anyone who doesn't demonstrate the same indulgence in the face of his unforced ability to recruit feminine tenderness from the strangest sources, a tendency that gradually became less disturbing as your Obby assumed more and more of the accoutrements of advanced age[47].

But even in the strappingmost epochs of his masculine purview which managed, so beneficently, a howling household in dysfunction with a sprawling chain of intermittently remunerative wholesale outlets[48]*, the everyday hesitations in his voice and eyes twanged in me chords of conscientiousness that overspattered whatever knowledge I knew of how extraordinarily murderous circumstances had already crucibled in him some very stern reserves of resources that could yet be called up upon in anytimes of direness. So why whack it that I so always presumed myself to be his caretaker even when his worldlywise competence so effortlessly overwhelmed my underweening flailings to underachieve in so many myriads*[49]*?*

[47] - which, by the wave, never ceased him from uptucking the big-legged housekeepers hired to reheat his morning bialys.

[48] *(while I upsurged adolescently in my bumptiousmost effrontery)*

[49] such as, for insistence, keeping gasoline in the convertible he bought me to drive between stations.

But somethings like that, as I came of sage, became a near commonplace in the subdivided shtetls of survivorland. **That burly truck driver with the nervous tic? He led armed men in partisan forests hiding children and elders safe deep under crunchy snows**.

That cigar-coughing seller of death insurance? He dragged informants from their grease-smoked kitchens and punched bullets between their anguished eyes under iceclad pines. **That raccoon-eyed librarian? Following the loud sounding roundup of siblings, parents, cousins, and urine-scented grandparents, she huddled her taut frame too tightly round a smothered baby niece in an empty cistern behind a frozen coal bin until the last loose heirloom was looted by friendly neighbors from her noosed family's ransacked farm.**

That saturnine shuffler? He never hurt a fly. He just survived. **That laughing harridan? They murdered her first husband and brood, but is now with new issue who've spawned crawling rugrats of their own.** That lanky bookseller? **That anxious landlord?** That chain-smoking stenographer? **That vodkamouthed claims** investigator? *That fleshy, pigeyed greengrocer?* **That lipsticked Tupperware Empress?** *That soulful schlubby housewife?* **That bespectacled nebbish who sells you magazines and breath mints?** *That brash know-it-all pisk with the racing forms?* **That flirty matron with the papery skin?** *That green mascaraed Mrs. Robinson?* **That eye-shifting, droopy little barfly?** *That unshaven platform stander at the station on all the coldest dark mornings?* **That sunburnt jolly beach ball thrower with sand spackled over the backside of his well-soaked Bermudas?** *That horse-voiced abuser of umpires two seats away in Spray Stadium?* **That overly distinguished gentleman who carefully offers you sports pages as he dips away from the donut counter?** *That flesh puffy arm with the nicotine-stained fingers below the rolled-up sleeve of the sloppy floppy green chenille sweater pushing, to untiring howls of abandoned laughter, a boisterous baby on the small children's swing-set in Roslyn Park one cloudsoft 1973 April afternoon*[50]?

---

[50] Sometimes it was almost a surprise not to see some blotchy tattoo on a casually exposed forearm. Once your mother inked bruised blue numbers onto us together both. Once I dreamt I saw one welted into your thin wing - and all I could do was count the wavering pin hairs dancing round it on your tender skin.

*And what if **THEY**, with undoubted secret superpowers, could, under the worse of circumstances, transform their seeming selves into basilisks of fortified resistance, surefooted ushers of survival?*

Better, in the Liverpooled beatification of the LuceLipped Yankee Century, to defer...

Better to defend. Better to condescend. They were now just pitiable fishoutofsands in the wide opening conveniences of North American Alta Vistas. But better to've never waded too deep into the dark waters that wastefully spawned their resilience. They were, for everyone's slipfooted sake, to be ushered, guarded, and nervously appeased to the absolute extent passible.

But enough about them, you, and Her and everyone else. Lemme talk about me!

Early on in me puerile bumptiousness of prepubescence I learned the inane potency of the comedic pose. That, never crushed by the slapping backhands of parental desperation though quenched (almost) forever by the sobbing wet betrayal of maternal tears, is but a pale preconception of laughter's dagger which was kept in me short sheathed until the heartbeat of your joyful coalescence below her, not at all age expired, fallopianed ovaries let me wield it willfully whenever it wasn't warnfully grinned between my gripping teeth.

From the very spit, every wit in me disallowed the idea of willful betrayal on the part of your Mudder's turnabout and her resulting insurgent uncertainty as to the advisability of your extenuating to term. If she had, perhaps early on, ratified one of her myriad threats to terminate your uterine subsistence, I might have undergulped on as was my wont when she periodically buried some named, though unbaptized, houseplant whose christened monicker, bestowed by her, gave it near family member status.

But if THAT was not to be – and YOU **ARE** – then the credit goes to her. And for bitter or for liverwurst, this is something you mussed never freegulp. Love is not always warm and buttery. And that's a hash lesion we all get spread on our toast.

* * *

THE EGG

Never had words
And no way to mind the ripples it pulsed through
water and air
Or the claw scratches it left in crumbled earth
Or the sudden fertile emergence of an again egg
But without words it found itself tuned
Toward what it had made
And the whole
It had pierced in the shill of the sky.

And as a partying shot:

What is it, my dear, that spreads us out of ourselves intermingling us with everything while also pulling us deeper and deeper into what seems some "source" while seemingly and sternly holding us so affirmably together in the ongoing rush of creation? You only have to ask John Coltrane.

Goodbye, my baby. I'm all over and out, jest like Tom Joad.

*

Forty-Two

Are We the Stories We Tell Ourselves We Are?

a yuletide melodrama regarding generativity

The Chelonian Screed:

Are We
Every idea,
every fact,
every particle,
every complex,
every twist and turn around of partial self-awareness,
an enigma self-protecting, self-protruding, self-expanding,
self-diminishing obscurity
swimming through its apparitions
encompassing everything?
WE ARE

We Are
Turtles all the way down.
Turtles all the way up.
Turtles all the way out.
Turtles all the way in.
Turtles merging and diverging.
Each encompassing every other:
ARE WE

Dramatis Personae

Dreamers

Gretchen Adele Ider: (Streamly Gredible)	A slight girl in the early stages of puberty.

Apparitions

Sarah Himmerman Ider: (Mummy)	Greta's neuroatypical mom
Avram Maximillian Ider: (Daddu)	Gretty's morbidly obese father
Moishe Saul Idursky: (Obby)	The Gred's paternal grandfather
Jacob Israel Himmerman: (Zeyde Z)	Griefle's maternal grump

Spirited Prop Chorus Members

Ezra Beelzebub Pounder:	A carnivorous animatronic reindeer
Archie McTannenbaum:	A fiber optic stormtrooper

***

I

The curtains open. Centerstage is a large couch under a soft glowing spot.

Lights slowly rise to 25%

Behind the couch, to the left, is a fiber-optic Christmas tree. Stage right is a fireplace above which is mounted an "animatronic" reindeer. (Maybe it's a deer or an elk with Christmas lights. Maybe it's Ezra Pound with antlers.) Downstage right is a folding chair and a small, but sturdy, card table.

Perched crookedly on the couch is a girl, small for her age and barely showing mature physical development. She's wearing pajamas and snoozing messily in a tangle of blankets and pillows.

The reindeer, in a clarion countertenor and with as much Renaissance flair as possible, sings Greensleeves "What Child Is This?" The Christmas tree runs through its fiber optic repertoire of color changes, shimmering, undulating, blinking, winking, traditionaling, and avant garding. Together, they will watch: ironically, opportunistically.

The singing trails off. An orange 90s-era iMac is slowly lowered onto the card table. The stage blackens. As lights rise again, a woman is sitting hunched and fussing over the glowing computer.

Lights dwindle again to nothingness as spots focus on the couch, the chair, and the reindeer. The fiber optic tree glimmers metallically.

Greta: Mummy? (*She stands. Runs a few steps, then stops short of the impassive woman.*)

Sarah: No dear. I just look like me.

> *Sarah remains seated, staring straight ahead, never making eye contact with the girl who, as the scene progresses, will occupy every point of the visible stage.*

Greta: But...

Sarah: I've never not loved you, you know.

Greta: I know.

Sarah: You just don't know it enough! ...But that's not your fault even if it is. No one ever does. I never did but, then again, this is just what ghosts will always tell you.

Greta: Mummy, why are you here? Are you going to stay?

Sarah: (*tendentiously*) I don't know the answer to the first question, dear. No one does. But the answer to the second question is 'yes' as far as you're concerned. I've always been a part of you since ever before you even seemed even a part of me. Of course, that means you'll never escape me...which will often seem regrettable.

Greta: No Mummy. Just sometimes. I'm sorry. I'm sorry. I'm sorry.

Sarah: Please don't try to make me cry, baby. But, crybaby, it makes me smile too. See? (*she does not smile*) Is there anything sweeter than what is you and me together like this? Is there anything more ghastly horrifying?

Greta: Oh Mummy. Can you stay here like this for a while? Just a little while? Will you hold me while I cry? That would be sweet. So sweet...It would have been so sweet!

Sarah: So sweet. Do you think I can ever let you go? Do you think you can ever get away?

Greta: But...

Sarah: I know. But you know you can learn to feel me–or that part of me that can, that does, that will–hold you– anytime you're alone and really need it? Other times you won't or can't notice. Except you'll never really know when you're hearing my voice, seeing me out of the corner of your eye, or feeling me brush near. I can never hold you any tighter than I ever had, or than I am now. (*She reflexively turns away from her daughter who aggressively seeks her gaze.*)

Greta: But sometime I want your arms. I want to feel your heart.

Sarah: You know my arms are crushed and crumbled in your box. My heart was a dark gust of oil-black smoke. You know it's everywhere with Caesar's last breath now. You know Carol Ann's a better hugger than I was ever. You know you will have girlfriends and boyfriends too. And, lucky you, you know <u>you're</u> not allergic to all your little doggydogs.

Greta: Ohhhh!

Sarah: Ohhhh. Sweet baby, you know what you got from me is relentless perseveration, the kind that could grind down rock diamond mountains. The kind that could grind down you because it ground down me. But you know you've gotten <u>enough</u> of me for little you. It seems so hard, but what could I ever do but keep a crushing cushion of hyper-charged space between us? It's softer now when it seems like it's there, isn't it? Isn't it? I know there was something of a blow when what I was passed out of your life. But wasn't it some huge form of relief? I can pervade you now without suffocation. I can evade you now without asphyxiation. There's nothing between us that separates us. We breathe together now. I know you can feel it. Can you feel it now?

Greta: Mummy!

Sarah: Baby!

Greta: Mummy!

Sarah: I'm always here. I'm sorry. So sorry, sweet baby mine. I'm always here. I'm sorry too. *(Her spot fades as she resumes typing.)*

Reindeer: You'll never get away. *(the Christmas Tree blinks mockingly and aggressively.)*

***

***

II

Lights fade to black, then rise to 25%. The tree undulates in blues, bright and darker. Lights rise. A heavyset man shambles from stage right. He visibly considers the possibility of setting some of his bulk on the flimsy table but returns to the right wing to retrieve a more substantial armed chair. He sits heavily and eyes the oblivious typing woman uneasily. He drags the chair stage left and sits again.

Greta: That you, Daddu?

Abe: You were spectating Jackoff Marleybone maybe?

Reindeer: Blah! Scumbug!

Greta: *(after standing and taking a few steps toward him)* Oh, stoopid Doodoo, I just saw mudder.

Abe: I'm sorry, baby. I'd do my bestest to keep in between... But she loves you so savagely, so Duke Ellington madly. Don't you know that now?

Greta: *(standing strong in a calm, deliberate voice, part angry, part playful, part agonized)* I'm sooo livid at you, dupey doo. How could you leaf me like dat, ya fat bastid? I got no mudder! You shooddah been nextra careful after then, shouldn't you of?

Abe: *(covering his ears, though she never raised her voice)* Don't wail Babycakes! Don't WHALE like dat! I'm no Jonah. I'm too hard to swallow! And when you gonna get off this couch here? *(He rises and tries to gesture the standing girl to him.)* Why don't you get out a little bit now and den? Hah? All the cute little girlz are dying dare hair blue, not dat I want ya to be a French kissing lustbeein or nuttin.

Greta: *(jumping back on the couch)* I'm not ducking never gonna get off it! I don't hafta. If Carol Ann doesn't like it, I could buy this house out from under her if I wanted to. No thanks to you.

Abe: Yeah baby. Yeah, <u>Baby</u>! Money isn't everything, but it sure helps to flip people off. Ya gonna buy new puppies when these mutts bite the dust? You could have them freeze-dried and animintronned, I souphose. *(He sits next to her.)*

Greta: *(snuggling to him)* Daddu. Daddu. Daddy, can you tell me something not stupid and true?

Reindeer: But don't ask for <u>too</u> much...

Abe: Sweetie Sweetie Sweetie. Can't it be one or duh nuther?

Greta: *(pushing him away – and wailing this time)* Daaaad!

Abe: Don't wail sweet baby. Jeesh, it's scrutiating! Let me try. Let me try, though I dunno what good it'll do.

Greta: Daddu? Please? And no ducking turtles, ok?

Abe: *(hurt)* Ya gotta at least TRY to be fair to your old dead fat daddy...?

Greta: Daddu! Just...

Abe: Ok baby. Only for you...*(He walks and thinks.)* I'm nimprovising now... Ya think it's easier when you're disembodied? Art for Art's sake...We create ourselves. Moving and shaking. Trying to understand. Even a lie is a creation. Even a lie... And we smash into everything, each other, ourselves. Gravity is justice. Entropy is grace. It's all creation... Reproduction is representation. And no presentation is true though some seem sooo much closer. Somehow... To some. Anyway. Ok?

Reindeer: Everything clear now?

Greta: Ohh!

Abe: Ok baby?

Greta: Daaaad!?

Abe: Oh baby, don't cry. Remember. We all do the best we can. Let's help each other try harder. Ok? Ok? That's all I got now. Ok? Ok? I'd give you more 'ear. That's all I got. Ask no more my sweet. But it's *(he sings)* "*ASK NOTHING MORE OF ME, SWEET PEER. ALL I CAN GIVE TO YOU, I GIVE.*" ...Right?

Greta: Yes, Daddu. It is ok. But go away now, please? Ok?

Abe: OK baby. But, you know...

Reindeer: AND DON'T YOU COME BACK NO MOE. NO MOE!

Greta: I know. I know. You're always wid me, right?

Abe: You'll never get away, but that doesn't mean anything can stop you moving on.

Reindeer: Upward and gonward!

Greta: Ok.

Abe: Yes, Baby. Ok, sweet baby. Goodbye for now! But. Remembah... *(Jerry Lewis)* You can sniffle...You can snuffle...you can even shed a sweet baby tear now and den...but DONNNN'T cry out LOUD fercryingoutloud...

Greta: Ohhhh.

Reindeer: *(Jewy Ruinous)* I like it! I like it!

Abe: And you'll never getaway.

Greta: Ohhhh!

(Abe resumes his chair.)

Lights out except for the spot on the Reindeer who shakes his head contemptuously until the spot blinks out.

* * *

＊ ＊ ＊

I I I

Lights rise. The Christmas Tree sparkles incandescently in lurid golds, reds, and oranges. Stage left in pale blue light are two boys, alive and young in prewar Poland. One is shorter and solid: dreamy with books strapped and slung over his back. He wears his cap straightforwardly. The other, more wary and also more confident, is older, taller, and leaner. He's dressed roughly but as sharply as possible in a vest without a jacket. His cap is pitched back and truculently tilted. They disappear abruptly.

Stage right in blinding blue light are two concentration camp prisoners of similar physiognomies as the previous two boys. Both the softer and the harder wear rags with yellow stars. There's a blue triangle beneath the yellow star on the taller one.

They disappear and stage left in blue light two old men appear, one softer and gentle, the other tall, gaunt and haughty. They are dressed in faded black show biz tuxes and fuss a bit with their bow ties and cuffs until they are noticed.

Greta: Hi Obby. Hi Grampa Z.

   The two saunter jauntily towards the girl.

Obby: (backhanding the side of Fat Abey's head as he addresses the girl) Hi Baby.

Zeyde: Hello Kiddo.

Obby: Your parents been visiting?

Greta: Yes, Obby.

Zeyde: Vhut a pair: those two. (He grimaces with disgust.)

Obby: (to Z) They did the best they could. (to Greta) Remember that, baby.

Zeyde: So, it's our fault?

Obby: Nach! Nach! Stop it. Nobody's blaming you.

Zeyde: Nobody blames <u>you</u>. I got a lot I'm blamed for. A lot.

Obby: Can't you rest now? Let it rest?

Zeyde: I can never. Look at her on that couch. Think of my Benny. I can never get away. And I ask no forgiveness!

Reindeer: *"JE NE REGRETTE RIEN...."*

Obby: You got nothing to be forgiven for. You were young. You were strong always. And so proud and hurt. But if, somehow, someone wanted to forgive you a little? Wudd it kill you?

Reindeer: (Sid Vicious)*"TO THINK IT CAME TO THAT. I KILLED A CAT. AND MAY I SAY NOT IN A SLY WAY.."*

Zeyde: HAH! Vud it kill me he says? I'm only dead twelve months now, and vud it kill me he says ...Hey Moishe?

Obby: Whatizzit?

Zeyde: Aren't we... Sings *"TWO VERY ORDINARY PEOPLE...* Hah?...Huh? Huh? Huh?

Obby: Oy.

Zeyde: Come on. Vud it kill you?

   A soft shoe duet with Z taking the lead, but O succumbing to routine: line trading and harmonizing:

       TWO FAIRLY UNIMPORTANT PEOPLE
       MAKING OUR WAY DOWN AGING LANES
       TWO BARELY INCONSEQUENTIAL PEOPLE
       NOT BOUND TO COUNTING LOSSES OR OUR GAINS

Obby: Says you?

Zeyde: Watch Out!

       TWO RATHER UNPREPOSSESSING PEOPLE
       SURE TO BE IGNORED OR QUITE DISMISSED
       TWO VERY UNIMPOSING PEOPLE
       CELEBRATING QUIET REFUGE FROM THE BLITZ

Obby: Our New York safe haven!

Zeyde: You don't mean "asylum"?

       WE DON'T WANT TOO MUCH
       JUST KEEPING OUTTA DUTCH
       OUR BASIC NEEDS ARE FEW
       THE BARE MINIMUM WILL DO

Obby: The penthouse? …Still belong to you?

Zeyde: Vhut? Think someone else got a better view?

       TWO OLD AND UNIMPOSING PEOPLE
       FRIENDS TOGETHER SINCE WE DON'T KNOW WHEN
       TWO QUITE NON CONTROVERSIAL PEOPLE
       BOUND TO STAY ON GOOD TERMS TILL THE END

Obby: You know? Still glad I am I met you.

Zeyde: Just your luck, I'll bet ya!

       TWO VERY ORDINARY PEOPLE
       WE'VE BEEN PUT TO THE TEST

DESERVE OUR BIT OF REST
WE'RE MAKING OUR WAY
JUST HAVING OUR SAY

Obby: *Always gotta comment?*

Zeyde: *I should keep my mouth shut? Huh?*
TWO VERY ORDINARY PEOPLE
OF COURSE, WE NEVER KNOW HOW IT WILL END
OF COURSE, WE NEVER KNOW HOW IT WILL END
OF COURSE, WE NEVER KNOW HOW IT WILL END...

Zeyde: Thank you, Moishe. Thank you.

Obby: Dun mention it. Dun mention it. She liked it? *(to Greta)* You liked it?

Greta: I liked it! I liked it!

Reindeer: *(more mockery)* She liked it? She liked it?

Zeyde and **Obby**: Oh!... *(Almost shuffle into another chorus, but energy quickly fizzles.)*

Zeyde: Not so bad dis place, huh?

Obby: You think it'd be bad?

Zeyde: I don't distrust you, Moshe. You know dat...Nice couch ya got here, kiddo. I hear ya wanna buy it?

Obby: She dun need to buy nuttin here.

Greta: *(to Z)* How come you didn't pay them to take care of me?

Obby: You eat so much, do ya?

Zeyde: *(menacingly)* They make you feel a burden?

Greta: I am a burden.

Zeyde: *(dismissively)* They complain? ...You got recourse. Plenty.

Obby: It's not necessary.

Zeyde: Oh? So, you know vhut's necessary now?

Obby: (*to Gret*) Would it be so hard to make it as easy as possible for them? Vud it kill you, I mean?

Greta: I think I do my best.

Zeyde: But you're my daughter's daughter! A pill that's hard to swallow!

Obby: She's filled with light.

Zeyde: No, you and me, we're fields of light. She, the kid here,'s stuffed wid light and full of shit too.

Greta: (*pleased*) I didn't know you were a joker.

Zeyde: Wid your old man, you needed jokes from me? But (*Groucho*) since we're on the subject. (*to O*) Eh? Eh?

> HERE ARE TWO FUNNY MEN
> THE BEST YOU'VE NEVER SEEN
>> (*Z preens and points both thumbs at his own chest*)
> ONE IS MR. OBERKAPO
>> (*Z Nudges O and then nudges O again*)

Obby: (*Irresistibly pulled into the well-rehearsed routine.*)

> AND THE OTHER MR. CLEAN

Zeyde and *Obby* (*interchangeably and in "humorous" harmony*)

> WHEN THESE TWO CHAVERS MEET
> SURE IT PURELY IS A TREAT
> THE THINGS THEY'LL SAY
> THE THINGS THEY WON'T...
> AND THE SAD OLD WAY THEY GREET...

Greta: (*rushedly interrupting*) Thanks, anyway. For all the money!

Zeyde: (*now dead serious*) Just take care of Benny and don't wreck too much things with it.

Obby: Watch it now, Israel.

Zeyde: Well who can be too careful? (*to Greta*) Nice couch ya got here.

Obby: You take your time, girlie.

Zeyde: Like she's got nuttin' but time?

Obby: You want for her to keep safe, don't ya?

Zeyde: What keeps her safe from what's insider? You know that? Do you?

Obby: He's right, baby. This is no safe place. There is no safe place.

Greta: (*pleadingly*) It's alright for now, isn't it?

Obby: It's alright for now, isn't it?

Zeyde: Ach! Like I should know?

Obby: She found your daughter's journals. She's reading them.

Zeyde: Oy.

Sarah: (*under a spot in red*)

> July 7, 2004
>
> About as soon as we confirmed it was female, they told us it was deaf. We clap and click and snap and shout! It seems to respond, but they tell us it's profound. Her name is Greta, no matter what Abe says. And Abe says she's got all the makings of a CEO or a criminal mastermind. She's not even breathing 24 hours, but she's a force of will.

Somebody'll blame me if the infirmity is true. If they don't, I will. And she is a force of will, just not mine.

Just not mine.

And she isn't mine. Not really. If I were a Roman matron, I could lay it at Abe's feet, and let him *know* what to do. It would not be too late. We just have nothing to offer it. And the wolves will take her anyway because I see the wolf in her.

Abe is a sloucher. I am a foot-dragger and a door slammer, but she is a huntress beyond the sound of my voice. They'll equip her, they say, with an implant. But she won't be assimilated, hearing only tinny machine clicks of simulation.

Unassimilated and proud. I can see it already. Stronger than me. I see it. I feel it.

I'm still shaking from all the seizures and clenchings that brought her here. They are nothing I can ever again withstand.

What seized us? What made me seize him, that hulking clunk of a lunk to father this?

He says with his glum grin, I did the seizing, but something seized ME!

And now it's thrown me off like I threw him off that damp night and he said he felt cold but I bundled myself snug and pressed back against him only to take more of his warmth and keep him from mewling. And now I feel cold and wet and limp and lonely and lost, used up, and drained.

> What's more miserable than useless, pitiless, empty regret?
>
> It's all her. Everything that makes us is now her. Everything that made us. And, I'll never get away. We'll never get away. Once you have a child, you're pinned and pulled down forward forever by whatever seizes us ...by whatever never lets us go.
>
> What is it?

Zeyde: *(frowns, a tall thin Oliver Hardy)* Another fine mess they've gotten her into, you.

Obby: *(shrugs, a stouter Stan Laurel)* And don't forget... <u>Your</u> daughter! *(Waggles eyebrows and nods head affirmatively)*

They each try to initiate another lighthearted soft shoe, but . . . no.

Zeyde: *(outraged and furious)* Fur Shit's Sake! She left that around for the kid to find?

Obby: Vut's done is done.

Zeyde: *(resignedly)* Vhut's done is done. Don't ve know it.

Obby: Ahh.

Zeyde: I never advocated it; this so-called replication. Not one way or duh other. You?

Obby: We both fathered children. We both, more than one.

Zeyde: That's vhut our vives told us, anyvays. Who can know?

Obby: Something tells me...We knew.

Zeyde: Ahh. But most of it ve did when ve ver young. Those two schlubs? Old enough to know better. Ya gotta admit.

Obby: The kid! She's listening.

Zeyde: So. Vhuts done is done. Eh, kiddo? The problem is vhut vill ya do now?

Greta: Mummy! Ya didn't want me?

Sarah: Shush, baby. Who knows what they want?

Zeyde: That's a new one from her!

Reindeer: "YOU'VE... GOT... TO ...AXE SLENDERATE THE NEGATIVE! INCINDERATE THE POSITIVE! DON'T FISTULATE WITH THE MISSUS IN BETWEEN."

Abe: She wanted you. She wanted you. You're just too much to take in.

Sarah: And I could never take you in.

Greta: I'll never get away.

Obby: You can't tell someone they can or cannot bring forth a child.

Zeyde: You can't even <u>tell</u> yourself.

Obby: Things happen. Nobody knows why.

Sarah: That's not true. We can choose.

Zeyde: You can try to keep your legs together. They <u>say</u> it's not so easy...

Abe: Easier than keeping it in your pants.

Zeyde: Shaddup you widda sexism! (*Z is inordinately pleased with his own retort*)

Obby: In. Out. Not so easy.

Reindeer: (*ruefully*) I gots nothing folks!

Sarah: I could've aborted.

Zeyde: You could've?

Greta: Why didn't you?

Sarah: How could I?

Greta: You'll never get away.

Sarah: I'll never get away.

Sarah:

April 15, 2015

Everybody is so kind…

They send me messages of support…

They hug me. They step right up and pull me into their funk and hug me…

And at first, I didn't even know why…

It was like 'I was the last to know'…

Prisoner Functionary. Vorarbeiter Lagerpolizist. OberKapo…

Blue Triangle…

Criminal…

Of course. Criminal…

Collaborator…

Not Abe's father. Of course, not… My flesh and blood. They say.

…He tells me.

Sarah: Oh No! I don't have to go with what anybody tells me.

Greta: But Mummy. Don't you understand?

Sarah: Darling! What?

Greta: Mummy!

Sarah: What?

Greta: You'll never get away.

Sarah: What?

Greta: You'll never get away!

Zeyde: You'll never get away.

Obby: You'll never get away

Abe: You'll never get away

Greta: You'll never get away

Zeyde: You'll never get away.

Obby: You'll never get away

Abe: You'll never get away

Greta: You'll never get away

Zeyde: You'll never get away.

Obby: You'll never get away

Abe: You'll never get away

Greta: You'll never get away.

Sarah: Stop that. This is not funny.

Zeyde: Whaddit she say?

Obby: She says it's not funny.

Zeyde: Who said it was funny?

Obby: I didn't say it was funny. Abey, did you say it was funny?

Abe: I didn't say it was funny. Gretel, did you say it was funny?

Greta: I didn't say it was funny. I said she'll never get away.

Sarah: You're making this into a joke! Into entertainment. Into escapism.

Zeyde: Whaddit she say?

Obby: She said we wanna escape!

Reindeer: So there's somebody somewhere *doesn't* wanna escape?

Zeyde: What? She said that?

Obby: I think so.

Reindeer: *(as the Xmas tree blare blinks bright reds)* Nobody escapes from Stalag Opticon. ATTENTION! ATTEN-TION! Escape attempt in progress! Escape Attempt in Progress! To your Stations! Initiate Escape Attempt Protocol 17. Repeat. Escape Protocol 17 Achtung, y'all! Achtung Baby! We're gonna getcha, Bubbe!

Zeyde: You know. It just goes to show. Stupid has nothing to do with intelligent. My daughter? <u>She</u> was always in-telligent.

Obby: But stupid.

Zeyde: Oh yeah.

Abe: Stupid is emotional.

Zeyde: *(irritated. Uncle Junior)* Who's talking now?

Obby: My boy, Abey.

Zeyde: He got so fat? When he get so fat? Was it because my baby girl killed herself?

Obby: Nah. Started long before that.

Reindeer: *(Luis Prima)* The bigga the bettah!

Zeyde: It started when they got pregnant? <u>They</u>!

Greta: I knew it was all my fault.

Obby: No. It started before that.

Greta: Long before that?

Obby: Short before that.

Greta: So, nothing to do with me?

Zeyde: What did she say?

Obby: She said she's innocent.

Zeyde: She said that?

Obby: That's what I thought she said.

Zeyde: Like I said. Stupid is emotional.

Abe: I said that.

Obby: So? He can't say that?

Abe: He can say that.

Zeyde: I did say that.

Sarah: Somebody has got to be innocent!

Zeyde: What did she say?

Sarah: I am talking about injustice!

Zeyde: What?

Sarah: Injustice! Depraved, unforgivable injustice. Heinous injustice. Historically reverberating injustice!

Zeyde: Did she say 'injustice'?

Obby: That's what she said.

Abe: That's what she said.

Greta: That's what she said.

Christmas Tree: That's what she said?

Reindeer: That's what she said.

Zeyde: Injustice? Of course, injustice. So? That's the soup we swim in.

Obby: (*solemnly*) We finnless soles.

Zeyde: So much injustice. But we don't drown.

Obby: We swim.

Abe: We tread water.

Greta: Sometimes we drown.

Sarah: Sometimes we drown!

Reindeer: Sometimes *YOU* drowned.

Zeyde: So, you drowned? You weren't the first.

Reindeer: Won't be the last.

Zeyde: Huh? You know injustice is a funny thing. Or maybe it's me. I'll tell you one injustice that really stuck with me.

Obby: Oh Oh! Oh no…

Zeyde: I know. I know. They played music so much in the camps. Sometimes when they took the children with their mothers…?

Sarah: A crime against music. Against humanity. Against whatever is human in music. Against whatever is transcendent in music.

Zeyde: Whaddit she say?

Obby: She said 'transcendent'. But never mind. She's…

Zeyde: …<u>intelligent</u>. She's very intelligent.

Reindeer: But stupid.

Zeyde: Huh? No. The music wasn't the crime. If I could've sung for some of them, I'd uv sung. You do what you can do. If I could've dressed like a clown…

Obby: Oy. Here it comes now…

Zeyde: That's right! Joseph Jerry Jewy Ruin Us Levitch. You know who I'm talking about!

Sarah: Oh Please!

Zeyde: (*to Sarah*) Oh Please, yourself. You know <u>your</u> mother was a dancer. And I don't mean just with her feet. Before you were born. Before Benny was born. Benny? Remember Benny? (*in an Al Pacino-esque roar*) Who you were supposed to take care of? …But before Benny. We had our own Joseph Joey named after you know who. And he was born wrong. That's something what was said about it, anyway. He lived a short painful life and then he died. And, somehow it took the dance out of her step. Why? Every agony of his, she felt. Why? Of course, she couldn't help it. And even the agonies she wasn't sure he felt…Your mother, she felt. After that. She plodded on. She staggered on. She dragged on. She droned on! She had two more children. She had Benny before you, poor Benny. Poor Benny. Healthy as a horse. He'll live forever. *(to Sarah)* You, <u>you</u> don't worry about Benny.

(to Greta) You. You take care of Benny.

Greta: I will.

Obby: Good girl.

Zeyde: I know. But do it by dancing. Don't stop dancing! It's like chicken soup, but bettah.

Greta: I will.

Sarah: I'm sorry!!!

Zeyde: Don't be sorry. Your mother never showed you to dance. I never showed you to dance. You were born perfect. (That's something they say.) But you were born *after* all the dancing. Not a single defect we could see. Do you blame your mother for leaving you like she did?

Sarah: Sometimes. I can't help it.

Zeyde: Well, you paid her back. Didn't you?

Abe: *(to Sarah, but pointing at Greta)* Paid it forward, you mean.

Reindeer: And life is but a circle. It goes round and round.

Christmas Tree: What goes around . . .

Reindeer: Numbs around. Slums around. Dumbs around.

Sarah: So much injustice! I'm so sorry dear.

Greta: Mummy! I love you anyway. I love you anyway! You did the best you could! I'll always be angry at you, but I'll never not love you.

Zeyde: Everybody does the best they could. *(to Sarah)* There were times I saw you, I watched you, and I thought you might learn to dance.

Sarah: I tried.

Zeyde: You did the best you could.

Sarah: *(to Greta)* I'm not sorry I had you. I'm not. I'm sorry for many things I did, many things I was, many things I wasn't, and many things I didn't do where you were concerned, but not for that. Not really.

Zeyde: Yes, you were. Really.

Obby: Nothing stops creation. Nothing stops it. Nothing tops it.

Zeyde: And there's no bottom.

Abe: Turtles all the way down.

Greta: Stop!

Abe: Turtles all the way up.

Sarah: Will you please!

Abe: Turtles all the way out. Turtles all the way in.

Obby: OK. Ok now. Thank you.

Zeyde: Now shut up with the turtles, now!

Abe: But it's about endless infinite creation.

Greta: We get it. We get it… Already. *(Adding the Yiddishism as an afterthought)*

Obby: And there are no crimes against creation.

Abe: Of course, there are. Worse than torture, worse than murder is to smother creativity: to stifle it for one's own comfort: benefit.

Obby: But can you do that? Can anybody? Can one person do that to another? Sure, you can bludgeon, torture, kill, and maim. But if the creative force is there, impeding it, is only like a dam. The force still builds behind it. Like a spring. Like whatever squeezes out a geyser? Maybe it's the spring in the string of a bow?

Zeyde: Nah. Nah. Nah. Are *we* talking ubermenschen now? We? Super master race? You? To me? Nah. Nah. Nach!

Obby: But there's so much we don't know... If there's a creative force...

Abe: Turtle force!

O,Z,S,G: Shaddup with the turtles!

Reindeer: And what's so bad about turtles?

Xmas Tree: I like 'em. I like 'em!

> *Abe (in exasperation) walks over to the couch. He's followed by Greta. They are followed by Sarah and Obby. Zeyde watches them and then turns to the audience. The lights snap to BLACK.*

* * *

* * *

I V

Zeyde stands frozen in a bright spot. Eventually, he braces himself and (against his better judgment) strides downstage and launches into an aggressive, unapologetic, defense.

Zeyde: You do what you do. Somebody needs a smack, ya smack him. Ya smack on the side of the head, ya might get his attention. I'm saying nuttin new. He pays attention, he might live another day because somebody else doesn't notice him. Is it good he should live another day? Who am I to say? Ya smack him too hard on his hand, he breaks a finger, he can't work. Maybe he gets noticed. Maybe he dies. Is it my fault? Sure. *(Al Pacino-like)* I offer no excuse! I accept all blame!... *(calmly)* Maybe I try to help him. Change his job a little maybe. Maybe they don't notice. Maybe he lives? Maybe not. Is it my fault? *(Grimly)* Let it be on me...*(shrugs, confused, resignedly)* Or not.

> *(Z shakes his head. Staggers. Looks at the audience and tries to explain... to himself. The Xmass tree dims to a soft metallic glow.)*

Zeyde: You smack him too hard on his elbow, he can't work

and there's no way to hide it. He dies. That's it. I don't smack anybody, I get it. I'm dead. They got me where they want me. They can kill me or they can let the others do it.

Actually, who did most of the killing? Who was "hands-on"? You think it was them? Not all da time it wasn't. It was us. Think about that. Think about that. Not that I personally led people to the gas. I was spared that. That ...But if they ordered me? What would I do?...I'd probably do what was mostly done. Don't let them think.

> *(Obby shuffles towards him as if drawn*
>
> *by an irresistible force).*

Keep them moving. Scared sure. But not panicking. Was that a mercy? Sometimes maybe it was. Was it to save our own skins? Why sure it was. That's human too. Make the best of a bad situation. That's what we do. *(sweeping a daggered finger across to the audience)* That's what you do. That's what we do always. Make the best of a godawful terrible situation. ...Is making the best, making anything better? Not often. Maybe hardly ever. But maybe you work not to make it worst. *(to audience)* You? And if no?...

I give somebody a better job. That means somebody gets one more difficult. More undoable. I give someone some extra food. That doesn't *always (shrugs)* mean somebody always gets less. Not even me even though I ate good. ...Good? Relatively ...Relatively.

But I say it again. I give someone some nourishment.

That might make a difference for them. Maybe they end up surviving just because of one or two little humanlike gestures. *(to Obby)* You got that. I know you did. I'd know it even if you didn't tell me. I saw your pictures. You were young and looked it. Young, but not too weak. Good looking. Yes. The very type some would help. The type anybody would help if they could. *(to audience)* The type you would help if you had the chance. You couldn't help!

Now is that justice?

(Lights rise softly to show the couch)

It's almost something no one can help: help. Now just look at <u>her</u>. Sure, she's my granddaughter. *(to Obby)* She's your granddaughter. But that's not the only thing that matters. Is it? Sometimes you just gotta help. But does your help help? Help what? Help how? Maybe it just makes you feel better. Or not feel worse. Is it even better that someone survives? ...Is it better someone is born? We don't know. We don't. We're just part of the push. Even if THIS BIG WOOSH makes us fall to the side because... or we drop off because we jump–or because we just drop. Even then maybe we're helping that push <u>push</u> because we're not in the way anymore.

(to audience) Look at her. What's she gonna do? We don't know. Bring joy? Of course. Bring misery? Sure. Do I wanna see her happy? Sure. Do you? Of course.

> *(Obby places a hand on Z's shoulder. Z flinches, but accepts this.)*

Zeyde: *(to Obby)* Did you ever make her cry? I mean aside from dying? No? You were her good grandfather. You were her "Abba." You didn't have to. But it wasn't that way with your own son and his sister, was it? To keep them from harm, you hurt them. You did. I did. To keep them from hurting themselves. To keep the world from hurting them. To keep you from hurting them. You were closer to your children, weren't you?

Obby: Maybe.

Zeyde: Lotsa good it <u>diadem</u>, right?

Obby: I dunno.

Zeyde: But they'll tell you sometimes they want their... space. Don't they? They gotta have that. The children. The wives. The girlfriends even. Me. You. Isn't it so?

Abe: *(rising and barging in)* And the space between us is alive with its own consciousness, twisting and pushing and pulling.

Zeyde: Will you shaddup!

Obby: Not now, Abey. Please.

Zeyde: Anyway, you always had a lot of space to give her when you weren't taking up so much of it with your hulking bulk. And now there's infinite space between you and her.

Abe: Actually, there's no space now, ever.

Greta: *(standing up)* I'll never get away.

Abe: Do you wanna?

Greta: *(running to him)* No Daddu. I never do.

Zeyde: Not so far.

Reindeer: Not so far.

Sarah: But what I did was worse. You have to keep me away. You must. I didn't want to hurt you. I don't want to hurt you.

Zeyde: *(With every ounce of meaning and menace)* <u>I won't let you</u>!

Sarah: *(standing up)* What can you do?

Obby: I will try to stop you.

Abe: We won't let you. We all won't let you. And you and me are part of we. We won't let you.

Greta: *(reassuring and placating)* I won't let you. I wouldn't do that to you. I love you.

Zeyde: See? You don't deserve that. But it happens anyway. It happens anyways.

Greta: OH. I'LL BECOME A MOLE AND TUNNEL UNDER-GROUND.

Zeyde: AND I'LL BECOME A BULLDOZER. IN TWO SCOOPS YOU'LL BE FOUND.

Greta: SO I'LL BECOME AN ARROW AND QUIVER THROUGH THE SKY.

Obby: I'LL CONDENSE TO A SUPER CLOUD AND CATCH YOU SHOOTING BY.

Greta: I'LL BECOME AN EEL AND SLIVER THROUGH THE SEA.

Abe: *AND I'LL BECOME A TRAWLING HULL AND DRAG YOU BACK TO ME.*

Greta: *I'LL BECOME A SUNLIT BREEZE AND WAFT INTO THE AIR.*

Zeyde: *I'LL BECOME A BLACK VULTURE AND SOAR WITH YOU EVERYWHERE.*

> *The Christmas Tree dons a German World War II helmet and joins the dancing chorus*

YOU'LL NEVER GET AWAY (8x)

Greta: *THEN I'LL BECOME GRAIN OF SAND. HIDE SPAR-KLING ON SOME BEACH*

Obby and Z: *THEN WE'LL BECOME THE RISING TIDE WITH OUR GLOBAL SURGING REACH*

Greta: *THEN I'LL BECOME A BABY SEED AND SPROUT INTO SOMETHING NEW.*

Reindeer: *THEN WE'LL BECOME THE SUN AND RAIN TO PULL THE BEST FROM YOU.*

> *The Reindeer pulls in his head and emerges from the fireplace and, wearing a satanic medallion joins the Xmass tree as the other endman*

Reindeer and Tree: *YOU'LL NEVER GET AWAY (8x)*

Greta: *THEN I'LL BECOME A MIRROR SO ALL YOU'LL SEE IS YOU.*

Reindeer: *THEN WE'LL BECOME A SHORT-HAIRED GIRL AND DO WHAT YOU WOULD DO.*

Greta: *NOW WHAT ELSE COULD I BE? HOW 'BOUT A CHRISTMAS TREE?*

Xmas tree: *I'LL BE YOUR ANGEL AND YOUR STAR, AND KEEP YOU UNDER ME.*

> *Abey who has been resisting joins the chorus line right behind his daughter and places his hands protectively on her shoulders*

Abe: You'll never get away.

> *Sarah, who has been disapproving, disgusted, and outraged is now distraught. Greta runs over to comfort her. The men are disdainful*

Zeyde: *(To everyone including the audience)* But really. That little girl. Do you really think she's really something special? Really?

> *Greta leads her weeping mother to her couch.*

Obby: I can only answer for myself. And so of course, she is. *(to everyone, including the audience)* You want to give a different answer? Do you want to say that you don't know?

Zeyde: I only know what I always knew even if I couldn't even keep it with me inside me. Everything is special. Everyone is special. But what that means, I never knew and maybe never will. How can anything and everyone be special when everything is? And why say everyone? Why are people-humans so special unless everything is special–even what we only think of as nothing?

Abe: Because everything is one.

Zeyde: For the sake of decency and sanity, shut your silly
mouth! You're blithering!

Abe: I'm not. We just don't know what it means but that's
because we're in it. We're a part of it.

Obby: Ok. Ok: But tonight, we're all apart from her. We're all
for her tonight. We are all her tonight.

Abe: Don't try too hard to understand, little butt. Just try in
bits and bursts. In snips and snaps.

> *Abey and Obby go to the couch and sit on each arm.*
> *Z looks at them and sees no place for himself. He*
> *turns reluctantly to the audience, looking at them,*
> *and shaking his head.*

Zeyde: Understanding. Understanding. We talked a bit about
injustice, didn't we? A child is beaten for no reason.
Someone takes his food. Someone takes her candy.
Someone brands her face. Someone changes the channel.
Somebody is murdered. Someone makes them go to
school. Someone makes her pee in a pot. Someone never
gets a hug. Someone gets raped. Someone never gets a
blowjob. Someone doesn't get into college. Doesn't get a
job. Jewy Ruinous doesn't get to play Hold On Coughing
Cauliflower Feldman on The Day the Clown Sighed.
Injustice. Were the camps the greatest injustice? The
greatest genocide? The greatest cruelty? Greater than
Black Slavery from dungeons to sardine ships to auction
block to whipping block to generations of rape and
murder and torture and diminishment. We should be
more solemn about the crimes of Hitler and German
speakers than the crimes of English speakers in the

Transvaal, the Connecticut Valley, the Philippines, The Mekong Delta? Hiroshima?

A moment of silence we should have? For every child left cold alone in a crib for days untouched? *(to Reindeer)* Untorched.

Let me tell you something about injustice and why we'll never get away. I know from this because of something she read. *(to Greta)* That's right, almost nothing any of us say is nothing you don't know. Remember AIDS? When it started, we thought it was a scourge on the fagelas. We did. But it wasn't and it didn't even really start with them and their fairy ways. It came from a monkey, didn't it?

Greta: A chimpanzee. And I didn't read about it, it was on NPR.

Zeyde: That's right. How was that? What about dis chimpanzee?

Greta: *(She joins him upstage)* Some man in Africa ate a chimpanzee maybe right before you were even born.

Zeyde: *(with wolfish satisfaction)* That's right.

Greta: The man killed it for meat and its blood had the virus. So, he got it.

Zeyde: But was that how it started?

Greta: No. Maybe a million years before another chimpy ate two different monkeys with two different viruses inside 'em.

Zeyde: And how does a big bad chimpanzee eat a little bitty monkey?

Greta: He just catches 'em and eats 'em alive. They scream and scream.

Zeyde: The little monkeys scream and scream while the chimp gouges into them for some tasty organ morsel.

Greta: And they scream and scream in terrible agony. And that's how they die in merciless pain.

Zeyde: Is that injustice?

Greta: I dunno.

Zeyde: Is that injustice to the monkey?

Greta: It's pain and fear. Terrible fear and pain.

Zeyde: To the chimp?

Greta: It's food.

Zeyde: It's life. Does injustice exist to animals, the ones who are not human?

Abe: Reciprocity! Primates. Dogs. Other species recognize reciprocity and its violations.

Zeyde: (addressing the girl and ignoring her father pointedly) But does injustice make them suffer the way it does for humans?

Greta: I dunno. Maybe in a way.

Zeyde: The same way?

Greta: Not the same way. It might not be the same way.

Zeyde: Does injustice drive them to change?

Greta: I dunno. Maybe. A little maybe sometimes?

Abe: (butting in clumsily from a distance) Does it drive us to change the way we organize ourselves? I mean, does it do that more than greed does? Greed for power? Greed for money?

Zeyde: *(Heading him off at the pass.)* Greed drives injustice and awareness of injustice. So shaddup. And believe me, greed needs laws and "justice" to protect itself. But shaddup anyways.

Abe: *(joins them upstage)* But greed drives us more than justice does. Greed is more in the forefront.

Obby: Ok already. You've had your say.

Zeyde: Men have "issues." Other animals don't. Injustice is one. For the victims. For the perpetrators. For the benefactors. For the side liners. *(to Greta)* Do you think it's just you can go out into the frigid cold in your cute wools and fleeces while people who worked hard for years and years shiver in cheap vinyl jackets?

Greta: It's not fair. It's not my fault. *(She jumps into Abey's arms who blissfully cradles her.)*

Zeyde: No, and you could give away all your…MY money and not change a thing. It's up to the victims to change things. When the victims get strong enough, nothing can stop them. Then …maybe… somebody with privileges can help change happen peacefully, and, by the way, maybe keep their head on their shoulders…

Reindeer: Yes, it's just sooo simple!

Zeyde: Stories are about what is possible–even when all they do is focus on what is impossible. Try telling somebody something is impossible. Better do it carefully, or you've fired up a challenge in someone–even someone crushed empty of hope.

Obby: *(joining them)* Stories are about what is possible even when all they seem to do is distract. Let someone be told,

by himself or somebody else, that what they do is useless, and maybe the question is triggered, 'Well, what is
useful?' And you can't separate what's useful from what's
possible.

> *The reindeer and the Xmass tree, disgusted*
> *and repelled by this discourse, slowly retreat*
> *toward their original positions.*

Abe: Stories are about what's conscious and what's not
because there are always stories and more behind the
story. Let someone notice that, and they'll always be
tempted to *(reciting)* "*wonder whether and where hidden
their meanings.*" And nothing is meaningful unless it
touches on what is impossible and what is possible.

Sarah: *(barging in)* Stories are about love and loss and
emotion and fear. And they are about a search for
resolution. Resolution, culmination, climax, and closure.
Those are all about love and justice, and the inevitable
question, "How are they possible?"

> *Abey sets Greta down between them.*

Reindeer: *(Oliver Twist. now again mounted above the fireplace)* "*WHERE OR WHERE OR WHERE ...S'LOVE?*"

Obby: When Man has given up on justice or has somehow
transcended injustice, he has surrendered or surpassed his
humanity. For love, it is the same.

Zeyde: In the meantime, you will suffer.

Sarah: In the meantime, you will hope.

Obby: In the meantime, you will inspire.

Abe*:* In the meantime, you will struggle with love and the meaning of meaning.

Zeyde*:* It's regrettable.

Sarah: Extremely regrettable.

Obby*:* Whether you win a slim victory.

Sarah: Whether you surrender to gravity.

Abe*:* Whether you are dissolved by grace.

Zeyde*:* Whether you are destroyed by contradictions.

Sarah: It's extremely regrettable.

Abe*:* But inexorable.

Obby*:* Essential.

Zeyde*:* Inevitable.

Sarah and **Abe**: We're always with you.

Obby and Z: You'll never get away.

Greta*:* I'll never get away.

Slowly, Greta begins to walk back to the couch.

The XMass tree becomes traditionally traditional. The reindeer becomes traditionally inanimate.

Greta turns, doubles back, takes her Obby by the hand, and leads him to the couch.

They sit and snuggle.

Sarah resumes typing.

Abey bashfully initiates some soft-shoe with Zeyde who

gradually encourages him with his own steps of generosity and flair.

Abey stops and turns to Gretel. Sarah stops typing, stands, and turns to Gretel. Z stops and turns to Gretel. She snuggles into sleep. Obby rises to make sure she's covered. He tucks her in. He joins the others as they watch over the girl.

Abe, Sara, and Obby apply sad clown makeup to Z's face who pulls off his tux to reveal a camp uniform with a yellow Star of David superimposed over a blue triangle. As Z juggles, the others step away into darkness until there are only two bright spots: one on the sleeping girl, and one on the juggling clown.

Z's spot goes dark.

We hear Capella Deucis *and* Quercus *sing* Xicochi xicochi.

And the spot on the sleeping girl grows brighter and brighter until it is abruptly extinguished...

*

Referential Addenda

Credo Credulamus of unReformed DisOrthodox Chelonialism:

Turtles
  all the way down
Turtles
  all the way up
Turtles
  all the way in
Turtles
  all the way out

Acknowledgement: Worship: A Love Supreme

Turtles:
  infinite
  ubiquitous
  existing, absorbing, emitting, propagating, expanding,
  contracting, melding, unfolding,
  enfolding, suffusing, infusing, mutually trespassing, and
  endlessly blinking in and out on 8 edgeless dimensions
  of ceaseless creation
  densely distorted by the porous selves of our four-
  dimensional sense shells.

Turtles:

each a multiverse insinuating into every planck of every
universe
each enveloping all
each procreating ever new permutations through
fission, fusion, explosion, implosion
each ever changing
an infinity of contingencies
eight dimensional constellations of spiraling:

Johns, Pauls, Georges, and Ringos *(first)*

Raphaels, Michalangelos, Donetallos, and
Leonardos *(second)*

Coltranes, Bachs, Dylans, Mozarts, Gershwins, Joe Hills,
Primas, and Irving Berlins *(third)*

Michaels, Gabriels, Lucifers, Clarences, and
Tiny Tims *(fourth)*

Alfred E Newmans, Karamazovs, Yosasarians,
Blooms, Falstaffs, and Harry Potters *(sixth)*

Camus, Einsteins, Aristotles, Neitzches, Feynmans,
Snoopies, and Yodas *(seventh)*

Ringos, Georges, Pauls, and Johns *(eighth)*

Spiraling within and throughout all harmonies

Pursuance: Creation: A Love Supreme

Unexhausting in astonishment, salvation, climax, and
transcendence
Unremittingly creating

Psalm: Gratitude: A Love Supreme

Sea of Holes
Sea of Monsters
It's all Too Much
Nothing's Too Much: Just Outta Sight
You Know My Name

Look Up the Number

O bla Di
O bla Da

UIKEYINPUTUPARROW

Be Here Now

UIKEYPUTDOWNARROW

A Love Supreme

Awaiting on You All
Bohm Bohm Bohm Bohm boomerang

Picture and Photo Credits

Cover art and design:	Joe Panzica
Chapter One Particle collision	**Casey Horner** on Unsplash (processed through CLIP2COMIC)
Chapter Two Skates of Matter	Joe Panzica
Chapter Three Papa Francesco	**Ashwin Vaswani** on Unsplash (processed through CLIP2COMIC)
Chapter Four All illustrations	Joseph Anthony Panzica Jr. (Penay)
Chapter Five Sad Balloons	Joe Panzica
Chapter Six Big Bang	Joe Panzica

Chapter Seven "peppers"	**Iris Colors** on Unsplash (processed through CLIP2COMIC)
Chapter Eight All illustrations	Joseph Anthony Panzica Jr. (Penay)
Chapter Nine It happens to girls	**Monika Kozub** on Unsplash (processed through CLIP2COMIC)
Chapter Ten Dimensional staircase	**Ricardo Gomez Angel** on Unsplash (processed through CLIP2COMIC)
Chapter Eleven Box	Joe Panzica
Chapter Twelve Rural ruin	**Christopher Windus** on Unsplash (processed through CLIP2COMIC)

Chapter Thirteen Under water?	**Cristian S., Barrett Ward, Trevor Vannoy Talia Cohen, Laura Marques** on Unsplash (processed through CLIP2COMIC)
Chapter Fourteen All illustrations	Joseph Anthony Panzica Jr. (Penay)
Chapter Fifteen Down the Road	**Christian Spies** on Unsplash (processed through CLIP2COMIC)
Chapter Sixteen Piles of Books	**Darwin Vegher** on Unsplash (processed through CLIP2COMIC)
Chapter Seventeen Fast Convertible	**serjan midili** on Unsplash (processed through CLIP2COMIC)

Chapter Eighteen
Pier

Anders Jildén on Unsplash (processed through CLIP2COMIC)

Chapter Nineteen
Toyroom

Dollar Gill on Unsplash (processed through CLIP2COMIC)

Chapter Twenty
Edge of universe

Pawel Czerwinski on Unsplash (processed through CLIP2COMIC)

Chapter Twenty-One
A *Lebensborn* birth house in Nazi Germany

Bundesarchiv, Bild 146-1973-010-11 / CC-BY-SA 3.0(processed through CLIP2COMIC)

Chapter Twenty-Two
Backpack

Joe Panzica

Chapter Twenty-Three
Graveyard angel

Diane Helentjaris on Unsplash (processed through CLIP2COMIC)

Chapter Twenty-Four Diner	**Alexander Kovacs** on Unsplash (processed through CLIP2COMIC)
Chapter Twenty-Five Busy intersection	**Jens Herrndorff** on Unsplash (processed through CLIP2COMIC)
Chapter Twenty-Six Ringo!	**Alisa Matthews** on Unsplash (processed through CLIP2COMIC)
Chapter Twenty-Seven Butterfly or wolf?	**Hermann Rorschach** (died 1922)
Chapter Twenty-Eight Scissors	**Naomi O'Hare** on Unsplash (processed through CLIP2COMIC)
Chapter Twenty-Nine Fabs	**IJ Portwine** on Unsplash (processed through CLIP2COMIC)

Chapter Thirty Thighs	**Ryan Hoffman** on Unsplash (processed through CLIP2COMIC)
Chapter Thirty-One Harmonium	**Saubhagya gandharv** on Unsplash (processed through CLIP2COMIC)
Chapter Thirty-Two Rolling Pin	**Priscilla Du Preez** on Unsplash (processed through CLIP2COMIC)
Chapter Thirty-Three All illustrations	Joseph Anthony Panzica Jr. (Penay)
Chapter Thirty-Four Make Way For Ducklings	**Lisa Yount** on Unsplash (processed through CLIP2COMIC)
Chapter Thirty-Five Simone and Paul	Unknown photographer and **IJ Portwine**

Chapter Thirty-Six obit	Joe Panzica
Chapter Thirty-Seven Bird of Prey	**Joshua J. Cotton** on Unsplash (processed through CLIP2COMIC)
Chapter Thirty-Eight Hospital Bed	**Martha Dominguez de Gouveia** on Unsplash(processed through CLIP2COMIC)
Chapter Thirty-Nine All illustrations	Joseph Anthony Panzica Jr. (Penay)
Chapter Forty Xmas tree	**Osman Rana** on Unsplash (processed through CLIP2COMIC)
Chapter Forty-Two Antler Skull	**Datingscout** on Unsplash (processed through CLIP2COMIC)